Amplified Pyrite

a short story in the
RomantiSea Serenades
series

J.D. Harbor

Ebook ISBN: 979-8-9921213-7-7

Paperback ISBN: 979-8-9921213-6-0

Cover Design: J.D. Harbor

Editing: Mehkala Spencer, All The Proof Editing

Formatting: Nicole Kincaid, Naughty Nook PR

One

Trevor's phone buzzed incessantly against the nightstand, dragging him from sleep with all the subtlety of a fire alarm. He fumbled for it, squinting at the screen through one eye. 8:30 a.m. Checkout in thirty minutes.

"Shit." He rolled out of the hotel bed, feet hitting carpet that had seen better days. The room looked like a hurricane had blown through a costume shop, with two suitcases splayed open on the bed, clothes and sequined chaos spilling onto the cheap bedspread.

Fifty-three cruises. Nine years. And he still packed like he was running away from something.

Maybe because he was.

Trevor caught his reflection in the bathroom mirror and winced. Hair sticking up at angles that defied physics, a five o'clock shadow that had evolved into a full day's worth of scruff, and eyes that belonged to someone who'd been running on fumes for the better part of a decade.

"Trevor looks like he needs a vacation," he muttered, then started digging through the nearest suitcase. "Steve IS the vacation."

Muscle memory kicked in. Quick shower, skipping any ceremony with checkout breathing down his neck. Moisturizer. Hair prep. He pulled out the electric blue board shorts with neon lightning bolts down the sides, and the neon pink mesh tank that never seemed to wrinkle, no matter how he treated it.

The "Electric Aqua" wig came out of its protective case like a sleeping pet, all tousled waves with subtle rainbow streaks that caught the bathroom's harsh fluorescent light. Trevor set it carefully on the counter next to his eyeliner.

This part required precision, even when rushed. Especially when rushed.

The transformation happened in layers. He started with eyeliner, applying bold wings that would make his eyes pop. The wig came next, settling over his graying hair like a security blanket woven from synthetic fiber and dreams. Body glitter caught the light on his shoulders and collarbone. Finally, a spritz of tropical boldness designed to survive hours of selfies and hugs.

He yanked on the electric blue board shorts with neon lightning bolts, the same ones he wore for embarkation day every damn time. Paired with a mesh tank and flip-flops, it was peak Steve: beach club ridiculous and ready to get the vacation started.

Trevor watched himself disappear in the mirror, piece by piece, until someone else entirely looked back at him.

The phone buzzed again. Messages from the Mingle crew, all caps excitement about anniversary plans. Nancy had sent seventeen texts since yesterday. Derek had created a group chat called "STEVE'S DECADE OF FABULOUSNESS" with far too many emojis.

Steve straightened his shoulders as confidence settled into his bones. It was like coming home. In the mirror, he practiced his signature smile, the one that made strangers beam back at him instinctively.

"Showtime, baby!"

The words crackled with electricity, and Trevor vanished. Steve took control now, commanding the swagger in his walk, the sparkle in his eyes, the magnetic pull that turned heads and stopped conversations cold.

The Elysian Serenade waited at Miami's port like box of jewels ready to be opened, and Steve was the key. He exploded through the ship's corridors like a force of nature, his hot pink mesh tank catching the light, electric blue shorts with lightning bolts demanding attention from every angle.

"STEVE!" The cry came from three different directions at once.

"Welcome home, mi amigo!" Luis practically vaulted over the Topaz Lounge bar, abandoning two other customers to reach for the bottles that would become Steve's signature welcome drink. "The ship, she was not the same without her brightest star!"

"Luis, you beautiful man!" Steve's voice carried like music, that perfect pitch of joy and mischief that made people drop their conversations and turn toward him like sunflowers toward light. His arms spread wide as he approached the bar, and Luis leaned across to clasp his hands. "Please tell me you didn't let anyone else have my usual spot?"

"For you? Never!" Luis's grin was infectious as he shook up a concoction that fizzed and shimmered like molten gold. "The VIP section has been waiting."

Steve spun on his heel, scanning the swelling crowd. Strangers lifted phones, caught by the current of excitement rolling through the deck. A woman in her sixties whispered to her husband, "Is that him? The one everyone talks about?"

Steve was sunshine weaponized, infectious energy in designer flip-flops, the human equivalent of a shot of pure joy mainlined directly into the bloodstream.

"Steve! Oh my God, finally!" Nancy materialized like she'd been shot from a cannon, practically vibrating with excitement. At fifty-something, she'd appointed herself the unofficial mother of their Mingle crew, and seeing Steve was clearly the highlight of her week. "Honey, we've been plotting!"

"Nancy, my queen!" Steve swept her into a hug that lifted her feet off the ground, spinning her around as she shrieked with laughter. "Plotting? Me? Never!"

"Ten years, gorgeous! A decade!" Derek appeared with Mike flanking him like backup dancers, both of them grinning so wide it had to hurt. "Do you realize you're basically cruise ship royalty at this point?"

People exploded around him in every direction, not gathering but detonating like Steve was a magnet and they were all made of metal. Jessica, the twenty-something newbie, stood frozen at the periphery, jaw dropped.

"Jesus," she breathed to her friend. "Is he always like this?"

"Always," Tony, the seventy-year-old widower, said with a grin that took twenty years off his face. "Son, I was starting to think they'd shipped the wrong Steve. This place doesn't work without you."

Steve's laughter erupted as he threw back his head, champagne bubbles and summer storms given voice. "Darlings, you flatter me! But you're absolutely right, of course."

The crowd around them kept growing. Other passengers stopped their conversations, drinks forgotten, drawn by the pure electricity crackling in the air. Steve was holding court without even trying, his voice carrying over the ambient noise like it was meant for this.

Hours melted away in introductions, drink refills, glitter exchanges, and enthusiastic embraces that instantly bonded strangers. By the time the sun dipped below the horizon, first-night-onboard energy crackled through the Topaz Lounge. Steve had been in perpetual motion for hours, with zero intention of stopping.

Somewhere in the middle of it all, he'd traded out the lightning bolts for his nighttime armor: the zebra-print slacks, matching jacket, and enough glitter to challenge the chandeliers.

"LADIES AND GENTLEMEN!" Steve's voice boomed across the space as he leaped onto the nearest barstool, then onto the bar itself with the fluid grace of someone who'd done this dance fifty-three times before. "Your cruise director of chaos has officially arrived!"

The room erupted. Cheers and whistles crashed like thunder. Luis's grin stretched ear to ear as he slid a glass across the bar, a pink, glittering concoction bristling with umbrellas, which burst into flame the instant Steve laid a hand on it.

"To new adventures!" Steve raised the flaming cocktail like he was crowning himself king. "To new friends! And to glorious disasters that turn into unforgettable stories!"

"TO STEVE!" the room roared back. The familiar high swelled through him, the rush of being the spark they all came alive around, amplified a thousandfold.

Someone started chanting his name. Phones appeared everywhere, recording videos instead of snapping selfies, as if this were a concert worth documenting. Even the bartenders filmed while they worked, laughing at the spectacle.

"You want a show?" Steve called out, spotting the piano in the corner. "I'll give you a show!"

He vaulted over the bar with athletic grace that made the crowd gasp and cheer, landing in a perfect crouch before bouncing up with his arms spread wide. The piano bench became his stage as he grabbed the microphone.

"Hit it, Luis!"

Luis, somehow reading his mind, cued up "Good as hell" on the sound system. Steve's voice soared over the opening notes, and the entire lounge transformed into a concert venue. People were dancing on chairs, singing at the top of their lungs, waving their drinks in the air like lighters.

Steve commanded that room like he was born for it. Every gesture was theater, every note was perfection, every smile was a gift to someone specific in the crowd. He pointed to shy passengers and made them beam. He pulled Nancy up to dance and made her feel like a teenager. He made Jessica cry happy tears and Tony laugh so hard he had to sit down.

This was what he lived for. This moment when the whole room became a party, when strangers became family, when everyone forgot their problems and existed in the bubble of pure, concentrated joy he created.

The song ended to deafening applause, and Steve took a bow so theatrical it belonged on Broadway. "You're too kind, darlings! Save some energy for tonight! I'm just getting started!"

"Steve! Steve! Steve!" The chant started small but grew until the whole lounge was shaking with it.

Lila pushed through the crowd, tears of laughter streaming down her face. "We've got something special planned for the end of the cruise. The anniversary celebration to end all celebrations!"

"You know me!" Steve grinned, the spotlight making his glitter catch fire. "Always ready to party!"

But even as he said it, even as the cheers swelled again, an unwelcome thought edged into his mind. Trevor's voice asked: *What if I don't want their hall of fame? What if I only want to...*

"Come on!" Steve announced, drowning out the thought with movement and energy and the promise of more magic. "Let me show you beautiful people where the *real* party happens!"

He led his victory parade through the ship's corridors like a conquering hero, twenty-plus people following in his wake, all of them high on the contact buzz of being in Steve's orbit. Passengers stopped to stare as they passed. Some joined the procession, others simply watched with grins blooming across their faces.

Steve regaled them with stories as they walked, his voice carrying over their laughter, his hands gesturing wildly as he painted pictures of previous cruise adventures. He was a one-man entertainment system, a walking party that made the ship itself feel more alive.

Past the elegant dining rooms where servers paused to wave, past the boutique shops where clerks pressed against windows to watch the parade go by, toward the vibrant sounds of salsa music drifting from El Corazón. Hand-painted murals of tropical scenes decorated the walls, and the air grew thick with the scent of spice and lime.

"This, my darlings," Steve said, his voice dropping to a theatrical whisper that somehow carried to the back of the group, "is where—"

The words died in his throat.

The parade stumbled to a confused halt behind him, twenty people suddenly wondering why their leader had turned into a statue.

There, at the bar, dark hair catching the warm light from the papel picado strung overhead, was a woman whose laugh he would have recognized if he'd been dead for a decade.

No. It can't be ...

Time shattered around him. The salsa music became white noise. The chatter of his followers faded to nothing. Even the Caribbean air seemed to stop moving.

No, no, no. Not here. Not now. Not looking like this.

Stephanie shifted, and memory surged through him with cutting clarity. She radiated more than beauty: a composure that hadn't existed in college, the quiet blaze of a woman forged by storms and steadied by survival.

Steve's knees went weak. His zebra suit suddenly felt like a neon sign screaming LOOK AT THE FRAUD. The wig suddenly weighed a thousand pounds.

She was right there. Right fucking there, three yards away, and if she turned just a little more, she'd see him. See Steve. See the glitter and the performance, and she'd know that this was what Trevor Dean Barnes had become.

A cruise ship clown. A walking midlife crisis in synthetic hair and body glitter.

The thought terrified him almost as much as the possibility that she wouldn't recognize him at all.

"You know what, darlings?" Steve's voice cracked back to life like a radio being tuned, higher than usual, but he covered it with the biggest, brightest laugh he could manufacture. "Change of plans! We're going BIGGER!"

His entourage looked confused. Twenty people who'd been caught up in the electric energy of Steve's world suddenly found themselves being steered away from the promised land.

"Pool party! Right now! Come as you are, no changing clothes, no hesitation, just pure spontaneous magic!"

The group's confusion melted into excitement. Nancy gasped and clapped her hands. "Oh my God, yes! Like that time in Cozumel when you got everyone to jump off the pier!"

"Exactly like Cozumel!" Steve felt the lie catch fire, becoming real in the telling. "But better! Aphrodite's Pool is calling our names, babies, and when have we ever said no to Aphrodite?"

Jessica looked down at her sundress. "But I'm not—"

"Perfect!" Steve pointed at her like she'd won the lottery. "Pool parties are about the energy, not the outfit! You look gorgeous, and that dress is going to look even better wet!"

Mike was already pulling off his button-down shirt. "You know what? Fuck it. I'm in."

"That's the spirit!" Steve felt the momentum building, his panic transforming into inspiration. "We're about to create the most legendary first-day pool party in Mingle at Sea history!"

By the time they reached Aphrodite's Pool, the group was breathless with laughter, still riding the high from Steve's last unexpected pivot.

"ALL RIGHT, MY BEAUTIFUL CREATURES!" he shouted, spinning in a circle with arms wide. "You came to cruise! You came to mingle! Now we make waves!"

And then he ran.

"Last one in buys the next round!"

Zebra jacket. Wig. Rhinestone sunglasses. Every sequin still clinging on. Steve flung himself forward and cannonballed straight into the water.

"CANNONBAAAALL!"

The splash exploded. No warning. No time to think. Just instant chaos.

Mike jumped in right after, then Derek. Jessica shrieked with laughter and dove in fully clothed, sundress billowing.

One by one, the rest followed. Nobody stopped. Nobody asked questions. Velvet jackets and cocktail dresses plunged in alongside glitter heels, everything hitting the water like it belonged there.

Steve surfaced, soaked and sparkling, wig sliding sideways and eyeliner halfway to his chin. "WHO'S NEXT?" he shouted, spinning in place with a splash that hit everyone nearby.

Laughter bounced across the deck. A drink sailed into the shallow end like a relay baton, while a guest swam past in formal shoes.

It didn't matter. Nothing mattered except the moment.

"This," Steve shouted, arms lifted to the sky, "is how you start a goddamn cruise!"

This was the beginning. This was the show.

And Steve? He never missed an opening night.

Two

The Blissful Harvest buffet sparkled with morning light streaming through the floor-to-ceiling windows, casting rainbow patterns across the market-style food stations. Steve had positioned himself at a corner table that offered dual advantages: perfect sightlines to both the omelet station and the corridor traffic, ideal for people-watching and performance opportunities.

"Steve, honey, you're going to make me jealous of that fruit salad," Cami said, sliding into the seat across from him. She looked like she'd stepped out of a magazine spread, even at nine in the morning, her micro braids swept into an elegant updo showing off statement earrings that caught the light.

"Darling, everything tastes better when you're living your best life," Steve replied, gesturing dramatically with his fork. "Besides, I need to maintain this figure for all my adoring fans."

Lila appeared with a plate piled high with pastries, her coral-and-teal hair still slightly tousled from sleep. "Speaking of fans," she said, settling into her chair with feline grace, "I think I spotted three different people snapping pictures of you at the coffee bar."

"Only three? I'm slipping," Steve grinned, but his eyes were on her hair. "Speaking of developing reputations, looks like someone had an interesting evening. That's quite the bedhead, gorgeous."

Lila ran her fingers through her hair with a satisfied smile. "Actually, I met a lovely lady at El Corazón after you led your parade away. Turns out some of us know how to have fun without jumping in pools fully clothed."

"Touché," Steve laughed, raising his coffee cup in salute. "And here I thought I was the only one making memorable connections."

Maude joined them last, moving with the unhurried elegance of someone who never felt the need to rush. As the Mingle at Sea host, she had that natural authority that made people gravitate toward her, but she wore it lightly, like a favorite dress.

"Good morning, beautiful souls," she said, her voice carrying that hint of an accent Steve had never quite placed. "I hope the sea treated you well last night."

"Better than it treated the pool deck," Cami laughed. "I heard the cleaning crew was not thrilled with our aquatic festivities."

Steve felt a small spike of anxiety but buried it under a laugh. "Details, darling. When you're creating magical moments, someone has to sweep up the glitter."

"Steve! That was incredible last night!"

They turned to see Tony making his way toward them, practically bouncing with an excitement that was completely at odds with his usual reserved demeanor.

"Awesome pool party," he said, extending his hand for a fist bump. "I haven't felt that young in years. You're like the Pied Piper of good times."

"Just doing my part to ensure everyone has an unforgettable vacation," Steve replied, his smile shifting into full wattage. "Hope you dried off eventually!"

"Barely!" Tony laughed. "Nancy's still finding glitter in her hair. She says it's like magical fairy dust."

As he walked away, still grinning, Steve felt that warm rush of being exactly who everyone needed him to be. Maude was watching him with those knowing eyes, and he cranked his smile up another notch.

"You collect people like shells on the beach," she observed quietly. "Each one different, each one treasured for a moment."

"Life's too short not to spread a little sunshine," Steve said lightly, though the edge in her tone had him worrying at the napkin until it frayed.

"Even the most colorful fish need quiet waters sometimes," Maude said, her voice gentle but pointed.

"I don't know what you mean, gorgeous. I'm exactly where I belong."

Cami leaned forward, her dark eyes studying Steve's face. "You know what I love about you? You commit to the bit. But the best performers know when to take a bow."

"Who said anything about performing?" Steve's laugh came out a little too bright, a little too quick.

Lila doodled shapes across her napkin, her eyes flicking to Steve between strokes. "You ever notice how murals change with the light?

Same art, same wall, yet morning sun reveals details that vanish at sunset."

"Are you three ganging up on me?" Steve asked, but his tone was fond. "Because if this is an intervention, I should warn you: I'm much too fabulous to be fixed."

"Nobody's trying to fix you, honey," Maude said softly. "We're just … appreciating the artwork."

Steve was exposed in a way that had nothing to do with his rockstar persona. These women noticed more than he wanted, and he wasn't sure he could handle what that might be.

"Well, I appreciate you appreciating me," he said, standing and gathering his jacket. "Ready to show this ship how trivia is supposed to be done?"

They were walking toward the Sea Shanty for morning trivia when Steve's world tilted sideways.

There, near the pool area, dark hair catching the morning light, was Stephanie.

She was laughing at a friend's remark, her head thrown back in unguarded delight. The sound carried across decades and left Steve frozen. She looked radiant. Confident. Free.

"You know what, ladies?" Steve heard himself say, his voice coming from somewhere far away. "You go ahead, I'll catch up."

"You sure?" Cami asked, but she was already moving toward the trivia venue.

"Just want to check on something first," Steve said, hoping his smile looked natural. "Don't let them start without me."

The three women continued , and Steve stood frozen in the corridor, watching Stephanie and her friends settle into lounge chairs around Aphrodite's Pool. His heart hammered against his ribs.

She doesn't know you're here. She probably doesn't even remember you exist.

But what if she did? What if she looked at him and saw ... Trevor?

Steve forced himself to move, but his body betrayed him, turning toward the pool bar instead of following his friends. His hands shook as he approached the bartender.

"What'll it be?" The bartender was wiping down glasses with practiced efficiency.

"Shot of tequila," Steve said, his voice steadier than he felt. "Make it a good one."

Carlos raised an eyebrow but poured a generous shot of top-shelf tequila. Steve threw it back in one smooth motion, the burn grounding him back in his body.

You're being ridiculous. You're Steve. You charm everyone. This is just another conversation.

But as he watched Stephanie laugh with her friends, the sun catching the highlights in her hair, Steve felt a barrier inside him slip. She looked unburdened, alive in a way that pierced him and left him aching.

Just a friendly conversation. Test the waters. She won't know.

Steve straightened his shoulders, the liquid courage working its magic. The tequila was doing its job, his confidence returning like a tide rolling in.

She doesn't know. She can't know.

He walked toward their table with the easy swagger that had served him well for nine years, his smile sliding into place like a well-worn mask.

"Hey, gorgeous," he said, stopping at their table with practiced casualness. "Mind if I steal some sunshine?"

Stephanie looked up, and Steve's pulse stumbled. Up close, her eyes were exactly as he remembered: warm brown with flecks of gold, intelligent and kind.

"Well, hello there," she said, her voice carrying a slight smile. "I don't think the sun belongs to anyone, but you're welcome to share it if you promise not to outshine the rest of us."

"I'm Steve," he said, extending his hand. "And you beautiful ladies are?"

"Stephanie," she replied, her handshake firm and warm. "And these are my friends : Rachel, Becca, and Angela."

No flicker of recognition. No pause. Just polite interest and that spark of wit he remembered.

His shoulders relaxed. *She doesn't know. Of course, she doesn't know.*

"Pleasure to meet you all," he said, his charm clicking into overdrive. "First time on the Elysian Serenade?"

"First time cruising at all," Becca said, her enthusiasm infectious. "We're celebrating Stephanie's freedom from a cheating ex-husband."

"Becca!" Stephanie protested, but she was laughing. "What she means is, we're celebrating new beginnings and the fact that I no longer have to pretend to like golf."

"Well, then we're celebrating the right thing," Steve said, flashing an unguarded grin. "New beginnings deserve champagne and sunshine. Speaking of which ..." He motioned to Carlos, who was already lining up a round. "Ladies, consider this your official welcome to the high seas."

The chatter spun on without effort, and Steve found himself surprised by how much he liked their company. Rachel was sharp and witty, a lawyer who could volley quips right back at him. Becca radiated sunshine, her energy lighting up the table. Angela stayed quieter, but her well-placed remarks showed she caught more than most.

And Stephanie ... Stephanie was magnetic for reasons beyond performance. She was there, unguarded, vivid in a way that tightened through him, stirring feelings he had no words for.

"So what's your story, Steve?" Stephanie asked, settling back in her chair. "Are you the ship's entertainment or just naturally this charming? Because if it's natural, I'm going to need your secrets."

"Naturally charming, obviously," Steve said, his laugh coming easier now. "Though I've been known to provide entertainment when the mood strikes."

"I bet you have," she said, her eyes twinkling with mischief. "You've got that 'I once started a conga line at a wedding' energy."

They talked about the ship, about travel, about the strange freedom of being surrounded by water with nowhere to go but forward. As the conversation flowed, Steve's frame eased, his performance slipping into a more relaxed rhythm.

"You know," Stephanie said, "there's something about cruise ships that makes you feel like you can be anyone you want to be. Like a floating costume party where everyone's invited."

"Or discover who you really are," Steve replied, and immediately regretted it. Too close to the truth.

"Exactly," she said, her eyes lighting up. "It's like ... permission to try on different versions of yourself. Though some of us are still figuring out which version fits best."

She's talking about you. She knows.

But when he looked at her face, she was just animated about the philosophical point, not making any personal connections.

"Of course," Steve said, his voice carefully light, "some of us are perfectly happy with the version we already are."

"Are we, though?" Stephanie asked, her tone playful but pointed. "I mean, how do we know we're not just ... playing roles we got used to? Like method actors who forgot they were acting?"

Stop. Stop talking. Change the subject.

Stephanie's laugh rang out at Becca's joke before Steve could redirect. It was so open, so unfiltered, that his own laughter rose to meet it—no trace of the polished performance he'd honed for years, just a sound pulled from the part of him he rarely let out.

Trevor's laugh, broke free.

Stephanie paused mid-sentence, her eyes narrowing slightly as she studied his face.

Shit.

"This is going to sound crazy," she said slowly, "but you look really familiar. Have we met before?"

Steve's world exploded into panic. His smile faltered for just a microsecond before he forced it back into place, cranking the wattage up to eleven.

"Gorgeous, I get that a lot!" he said, his laugh too loud, too bright. "Must be the cruise ship lighting! It makes everyone look like a movie star."

"No, it's not that," Stephanie said, her brow furrowing. "It's something about your eyes. And that laugh … I swear I've heard it before. Like an echo I can't pin down."

She knows. She fucking knows.

"Well, I *am* pretty unforgettable," Steve said, his gestures becoming more animated, his voice more projected. "Ask anyone on this ship! I'm basically cruise ship royalty at this point."

"Stephanie, you say that about everyone," Rachel laughed. "Remember when you were convinced our waiter in Miami was your high school lab partner?"

"That was different," Stephanie protested, but her eyes stayed on Steve. "And I was right about the waiter, by the way. He remembered me once I mentioned the frog dissection incident."

"Speaking of unforgettable," Steve said, pulling out his phone, "we need documentation of this moment! Ladies, group photo!"

He managed to redirect the conversation into selfies and drinks orders, but he could feel Stephanie's eyes on him, studying his face like she was trying to solve a puzzle. Every time he looked at her, she was watching him with that same confused expression.

She's going to figure it out. She's going to remember.

Steve's performance kicked into overdrive. More jokes, more charm, more of everything, trying to bury Trevor so deep that no amount of scrutiny could find him.

"You know," Stephanie said during a lull in the conversation, "I have the strangest feeling we've met before. Maybe not here, but somewhere. It's like trying to remember a dream. You know it happened, but the details keep slipping away."

"Honey, if we'd met before, I would definitely remember," Steve said, his voice strained at the edges. "Trust me, I never forget a beautiful face."

"It's not about remembering faces," she said quietly, her head tilted as she studied him. "It's about … energy. The way you laugh. The way you gesture when you're excited. It's so familiar I can almost taste it."

Stop. Please stop.

"Stephanie, you're being weird," Becca said, laughing. "Just enjoy the cute guy who's buying us drinks."

"I'm not being weird, I'm being thorough," Stephanie replied with a grin. "It's a lawyer thing. I don't let mysteries go unsolved."

"Excuse me, Steve?" A British accent cut through the conversation. "Could I have a word?"

Steve turned to see Graham approaching, his security uniform crisp despite the heat, his expression professionally neutral.

"Uh oh," Steve said with exaggerated concern, flashing the women his most charming smile. "When the head of security knows you by name, that's either really good or really bad. Ladies, I'll see you around!"

As Graham led him away from the table, Steve glanced back to find Stephanie still watching him, her expression puzzled, her eyes searching his face for something.

She doesn't know. She can't know.

But even as he followed Graham to a quiet corner of the pool deck, Steve's heart was hammering with the certainty that his carefully constructed world was starting to crack.

"Steve, we need to talk about last night's pool party," Graham said, his tone professional but not unkind.

"Graham!" Steve's charm clicked back into place, grateful for the distraction. "Come on, it was just a little spontaneous fun!"

"It took the maintenance team hours to clean up this morning," Graham continued. "Formal wear debris, makeup residue, enough glitter to stock a craft store. We had to replace the filters because of you."

"Everyone had a blast!" Steve protested, his gestures animated. "Sometimes you've got to live a little! That's what vacation is for!"

"I get that you're just having a good time," Graham said, his voice patient. "But we have protocols. Just keep the spontaneous parties to designated areas, yeah?"

"Of course, of course," Steve said, his smile working its magic. "You know I respect the rules. I'm all about guest satisfaction within reasonable parameters."

Graham studied him for a moment, then nodded with an audible sigh. "I'll let you get back to your fun, but I'll be watching you."

But as Steve walked away from Graham, he didn't head back toward Stephanie's table. Instead, he moved toward the ship's interior, toward the safety of the planned activities and the Mingle group.

She doesn't know. She thinks I look familiar, but she doesn't know.

Twenty-two years. Completely different appearance. Trevor Barnes had been forgettable even then, one face among hundreds in the lecture hall, one awkward college boyfriend among several.

If she knew, she would have given him certainty.

At the entrance to the ship's interior, Steve paused. Longing tugged him back toward the pool, to where Stephanie sat with her friends.

She was still there, still beautiful, still laughing. Even from a distance, he caught the way her attention skimmed the crowd, searching for him.

She doesn't know. She can't know.

But as Steve disappeared into the ship's corridors, heading back toward the safety of his chosen family and their planned activities, he couldn't shake the feeling that his nine-year performance had just hit its first real snag.

Three

The tender boat cut through turquoise water toward the private Bahamian island, and Steve's shoulders straightened with each wave they crossed, confidence flowing back into his posture.

The island appeared ahead like a postcard come to life: pristine white sand, swaying palms, and coral umbrellas bright against the shore. Steve could already see passengers staking out spots on the beach, the whole scene glittering under the Caribbean sun.

"Now this," Steve announced to his group as they approached the dock, "is what I call a proper vacation day."

Derek and Mike were pressed together on the boat's bench, Mike's head on Derek's shoulder as the island grew larger. Only a couple of days into the cruise, and they had already been shipped by the entire group. Cami sat across from them, snapping photos of the approaching paradise. Lila had claimed a spot at the bow, her coral-and-teal hair whipping in the breeze.

They disembarked onto the dock, Steve naturally taking point as they made their way onto the beach. The sand was warm between his toes, and the salt air filled his lungs as he surveyed their options.

"Alright, beautiful people," he called out, spreading his arms wide. "I'm thinking we claim that prime real estate over there." He pointed toward a cluster of coral-colored umbrellas near the volleyball net. "Perfect view, perfect breeze, and close enough to the action if we want to show these other passengers how it's done."

As they settled into their beach chairs, Steve felt that familiar rush of being exactly where he belonged. Derek and Mike immediately claimed a double lounger, while Cami began applying sunscreen.

"So," Steve said, rubbing his hands together as he eyed the volleyball net, "who's ready for some friendly competition?"

"Count us in," Derek said, not moving from his position next to Mike. "In about an hour. Maybe two."

"I'm game," Cami said, looking up from her sunscreen application.

"Lila?" he asked.

"Why not?" she replied, not looking up from her sketch. "Someone needs to keep you humble."

Steve grinned and jogged toward the volleyball net, where ship staff had set up the court perfectly. The sand was level, the net was the right height, and the backdrop of palm trees and turquoise water was Instagram-worthy. More importantly, volleyball would let him shine in all his athletic glory.

Within minutes, he'd organized teams from the Mingle group. Derek and Mike eventually roused themselves to play, though their version of "competitive volleyball" involved more laughter than actual athletic prowess. Cami proved true to her word. She had serious skills and a wicked serve that caught everyone off guard.

Steve was in his natural element, calling plays, encouraging teammates, and making athletic moves that looked effortless but showcased years of actual skill. His high school and college volleyball experience showed in every play, muscle memory preserving one of the few things Trevor had genuinely excelled at.

"Okay, Steve, we get it," Derek called out after Steve made a particularly spectacular diving save. "You're an athlete. Stop making the rest of us look bad."

"Can't help it if I'm naturally gifted," Steve replied with exaggerated modesty, dusting sand off his chest. "It's a burden, really."

The game was in full swing when Steve spotted them. Stephanie and her three friends had claimed a spot near the shoreline, close enough that he could see them clearly but far enough that it didn't feel threatening. They were lounging on beach chairs, drinks in hand, looking like they belonged in a travel magazine.

Steve's serve faltered slightly, the ball going into the net instead of sailing over.

"You okay there, superstar?" Cami asked, raising an eyebrow.

"Just ... adjusting my strategy," Steve said, but his eyes kept drifting toward Stephanie's group.

An idea began forming in his mind. A brilliant, foolproof idea.

During the next break, Steve jogged over to where Lila was reapplying her lip balm. "Hey, gorgeous," he said casually, "think you can give me some serious heat on your next serve?"

Lila looked at him curiously. "What kind of heat are we talking about?"

Steve gestured subtly toward Stephanie's group. "The kind that sends the ball flying over toward those loungers. I need a good excuse to go introduce myself to our fellow cruise guests."

Understanding dawned in Lila's eyes, and she grinned. "Ah, I see. Strategic ball placement."

"Exactly. Think you can make it look natural?"

"Honey, that's what I do." She stretched her arms above her head, loosening up. "One perfectly imperfect serve coming up."

Steve rejoined the game, positioning himself for the retrieval mission. Lila took her position at the back line, the ball balanced in her palm as she prepared to serve.

"This one's going to be special," she announced to the team with a wink that only Steve caught.

Lila's serve was perfectly executed, clearing the net with power to spare and angling precisely toward the shoreline where Stephanie's group was lounging. Steve immediately gave chase, calling out theatrical apologies as he ran.

"Sorry! Sorry! Rogue ball coming through!"

The ball landed in the sand about three feet from Stephanie's chair, bouncing once before rolling to a stop near her feet. Steve jogged up, his most charming smile in place.

"Ladies, I am so sorry about that," he said, slightly breathless from the run. "My teammate got a little enthusiastic with her serve."

Stephanie looked up from her book, sunglasses pushed into her hair, and Steve froze. Her smile was easy, real in a way that shook him harder than any spotlight moment.

"No worries," she said with a smile. "Occupational hazard of beachside lounging."

"Hey, Stephanie, right?" he said, extending his hand as he picked up the ball.

"Yeah, and you're Scott, yes?"

"Steve, but close enough," he corrected her. "Since I interrupted your relaxation, how about I make it up to you? We could use more players if you're interested."

Rachel, the sharp-eyed lawyer, looked intrigued. "Beach volleyball? It's been a while, but sure."

"I'm in," Becca added enthusiastically. "This is exactly the kind of vacation activity I was hoping for."

Angela nodded her agreement, and all eyes turned to Stephanie.

"Why not?" she said, standing and brushing sand off her legs. "Just so you know , though, I played in college, too."

"Perfect," Steve said, his grin widening. "Follow me, ladies. Let me introduce you to the gang."

Steve savored the familiar thrill of orchestrating the perfect social moment as they approached the volleyball court. Yesterday had confirmed what he'd hoped: his disguise was bulletproof. Stephanie saw Steve , the cruise character, and nothing more. Trevor Barnes remained safely invisible, allowing him to enjoy this interaction with complete confidence.

The introduction unfolded exactly as he'd hoped: Derek and Mike charming Stephanie's friends with their easy banter, Cami immediately bonding with Rachel over their shared legal background, and Lila engaging Angela in a conversation about travel photography.

The expanded game took on new energy with fresh players. Teams were reshuffled, and Steve maneuvered himself onto the same side as Stephanie. Perfect. He could showcase his athletic abilities while keeping her close enough to observe.

And God, she was still incredible at this game. Just like in college, Stephanie moved on the sand with natural grace, her positioning perfect, her sets precise. Their old chemistry sparked to life as muscle memory kicked in, the same intuitive partnership that had dominated weekend beach tournaments now flourishing under the Caribbean sun.

When she dove for a save and surfaced with sand in her hair and a grin of triumph, the sight struck Steve hard. Not panic this time, but a heat that carried its own kind of danger.

"Nice save," he called out, and the way she lit up in response felt effortless.

The game intensified as both teams found their rhythm. Steve was in his element, making athletic plays that drew cheers from the growing crowd of onlookers, but he wasn't the only star. Stephanie matched him move for move, her competitive spirit revealing the same qualities he remembered from college, that focused determination that made her absolutely magnetic.

"Okay, match point," Derek called out. "Steve, don't mess this up for us."

"Pressure's on," Stephanie said, positioning herself for the serve. "Think you can handle it?"

Steve's competitive instincts flared to life. He crouched slightly, reading her body language, calculating the angle. The perfect moment had arrived to end the game with style.

Stephanie's serve was beautiful, arcing high over the net. Mike managed a decent bump, sending the ball toward the center where

Cami was waiting. She set it perfectly, high and outside, exactly where Steve needed it.

Time slowed as Steve approached the net. He could see the trajectory, sense the timing in his bones. Athletic excellence and perfect showmanship converged in this single, perfect moment.

As he jumped, a flicker of concentration crossed his face—the old tell from college whenever he tackled something difficult.

Steve's spike was devastating in its perfection, powerful and precise, and utterly unreturnable. The ball slammed into the sand with authority while the opposing team could only watch.

"YES!" Derek shouted, jumping up and down. "That's how it's done!"

The celebration erupted around Steve, but all he saw was Stephanie. She watched him with a look he couldn't decipher, her attention so fixed on him it left him unsteady.

She knew. Her eyes held complete recognition, not confusion or suspicion, but absolute certainty.

The realization hit him like a cold wave: she had always known.

"Great game, everyone!" Steve managed to say, his voice sounding normal despite the panic coursing through his veins. "Who's ready for drinks?"

As the group began to disperse, chattering about the game and making plans for the rest of the afternoon, Stephanie approached him with two bottles of water.

"Steve," she said, her voice casual but her eyes still holding that knowing look. "Can I buy you a congratulatory drink? You've earned it."

Steve's mouth felt dry as sand. "Sure," he managed. "That sounds great."

They walked toward the beach bar, making small talk about the game and the beautiful weather. Steve's mind raced, trying to figure out how to handle this, what to say, how to maintain the facade when it was already too late.

The beach bar was busy but had quieter spots toward the edges where they could talk without being overheard. Stephanie ordered two tropical drinks. Whatever combination of rum and fruit she'd chosen, Steve barely tasted them.

"Beautiful day," she said, taking a sip of her drink. "Perfect for volleyball."

"Absolutely," Steve replied, his performance mode kicking in automatically. "Nothing beats beach volleyball in paradise."

Stephanie looked around, making sure they were out of earshot of the other beach guests. Then she turned back to him, her expression sharpening into seriousness.

"So, Trevor," she said quietly.

The name landed with jarring force. Steve nearly dropped his drink, his body locking in place.

"Trevor?!" he asked, though he already knew. "I didn't think you recognized me."

"I knew it was you yesterday at the pool," Stephanie said gently. "I wasn't going to call you out in front of your friends. I figured if you wanted me to know, you'd tell me."

Steve felt the world tilt around him. "You knew? This whole time you knew?"

"We dated for two years, Trevor. You think I wouldn't recognize you?" Her voice was kind but certain. "That eyebrow thing you just did during the spike? You used to do that exact same thing when you were concentrating on problem sets in Professor Martinez's class."

Steve's carefully constructed world crumbled around him. All his confidence, all his certainty that he'd handled the situation perfectly. It had all been an illusion.

"God," he said, running his hand through his hair. "You must think I'm completely insane."

"I think you're having fun," Stephanie said. "There's nothing wrong with that."

Steve looked around frantically, making sure no one from his group could see them. "Look, Steve is just ... vacation . Trevor doesn't do cruise ships."

"Okay," she said simply.

"Steve knows how to have fun. Trevor is more ... practical, reserved." He was scrambling now, trying to maintain some version of the explanation that made sense. "It's not that complicated. Different settings, different energy."

Stephanie nodded. "I can understand that. Vacation brings out different sides of people."

"Right. Exactly." Steve felt a tiny bit of relief. "So Trevor's at home in Ohio, and Steve's here making friends."

"And Steve's the one who coordinates beach volleyball and starts pool parties?"

"Pretty much."

Stephanie was quiet for a moment, studying his face. "You won't tell them, right?" Steve asked, his voice urgent. "They know me as Steve."

"Your secret's safe," she said. "I'm not here to mess up your vacation."

The relief that flooded through Steve was overwhelming. "Thank you. I just ... this is how they know me. This is who I am here."

"I get it," Stephanie said. "Just ... don't feel like you have to perform for me, okay? When it's just us."

Steve took her in, truly seeing her instead of just panicking. There was kindness in her eyes, understanding, and a depth that loosened him with unexpected relief.

"I can do that," he said. "When it's just us."

"Good." She raised her drink in a small toast. "To vacation personas and old friends."

Steve clinked his bottle against hers, tension finally leaving his body since she'd said his real name.

"To old friends," he echoed.

As they walked back toward the beach, a change settled in Steve, leaving him no longer just Steve or only Trevor, but a new blend of both. After nine years of performance, someone finally saw both sides of him, and instead of disaster, he'd found acceptance.

It was terrifying and liberating in equal measure.

The group was sprawled across their claimed territory, everyone looking relaxed and sun-kissed. Derek and Mike had returned to their position as professional beach loungers, while Cami was engaged in an animated conversation with Rachel about something that involved lots of hand gestures.

As the afternoon stretched on, Stephanie's presence pulled at Steve's attention like a magnet. She sat with her friends, laughing at Becca's stories and chatting easily with his cruise family, but occasionally their eyes would meet across the sand. Each time, she'd offer him a small, understanding smile that somehow managed to be reassuring and unsettling at the same time.

She knew who he really was, and she was keeping his secret. But more than that, she seemed genuinely okay with both vacation Steve and practical Trevor, accepting him as a complete person rather than choosing sides.

The question bloomed in Steve's mind: what would it feel like to be both at the same time?

The sun was starting to lower toward the horizon when the various groups began packing up their belongings. The tender boats would be running every half hour back to the ship, and most people wanted to grab showers and rest before dinner.

As Stephanie's group headed toward their tender boat, she paused beside Steve's chair.

"Thanks for including us today," she said. "It was exactly what I needed."

"Anytime," Steve replied. "That's what vacations are for, right?"

She smiled, and for just a moment, he glimpsed the girl he'd known in college, the one who could make him laugh without effort and make him feel like his best self without any performance required.

"See you around, Steve," she said, with just enough emphasis on his name to remind him that she knew exactly who she was talking to.

As her group disappeared toward the docks, Steve leaned back in his chair and watched the sun paint the sky in shades of orange and pink.

Tomorrow they'd dock in Nassau, and he'd have to navigate uncharted waters: having someone know his secret while allowing him to keep it.

For now, though, he was content to sit with his chosen family, warm sand between his toes and salt air in his lungs. Nine years of careful performance could rest.

He could just be.

Four

The Nassau pier buzzed with organized chaos as seven massive cruise ships disgorged their passengers onto the weathered concrete. Steve adjusted his shirt, "Alright, beautiful people!" Steve called out to his group as they navigated through the crowd of tourists. "Paradise Island awaits! Who's ready to see what Atlantis has to offer?"

The pier shops stretched along the waterfront, their colorful awnings promising everything from duty-free liquor to authentic Bahamian crafts. Vendors called out in sing-song voices, competing for attention among the sea of cruise passengers. Derek and Mike were already gravitating toward a shop advertising conch shell jewelry, while Cami examined a display of hand-woven bags with the critical eye of someone who knew quality when she saw it.

"Steve, honey, you sure you don't want to hit the straw market first?" Nancy asked, her sun hat already slightly askew from the Caribbean breeze. "I heard they have the best deals on—"

"Trust me, gorgeous," Steve interrupted with a theatrical wink, "Atlantis first, shopping later. We've got all day to spend your money!"

Lila looked up from a vendor's display of colorful sarongs, her coral-and-teal hair catching the light. "How long until the water taxi?"

"Ten minutes," Derek called out, consulting his phone. "They're running shuttles every fifteen minutes to Paradise Island."

Steve swept the crowd, cataloging the lively sprawl around them. Families with strollers, couples holding hands, solo travelers clutching guidebooks. The usual cruise ship diaspora spreading across a foreign port like ...

His thoughts stopped mid-sentence.

There, about twenty feet away, stood a woman in a white romper decorated with blue tropical leaves. The lightweight fabric moved with her as she examined a display of local pottery, her dark hair catching the sunlight. She wore a delicate necklace and seemed completely absorbed in her browsing, oblivious to the tourist mayhem around her.

"You know what," he said, his voice slightly higher than usual, "you guys head to the taxi stand. I'll catch up in a second."

"Steve?" Cami raised an eyebrow, her expression curious. "Everything okay?"

"Yeah, just want to check something out," Steve replied, trying to keep his tone casual. "Give me two minutes, I'll catch up."

The group moved toward the water taxi area, their chatter fading into the background noise of the pier. Steve took a deep breath, straightened his shoulders, and walked toward the pottery display with as much confidence as he could muster.

"Excuse me, do you know where I can find a new hat?"

Stephanie turned, and Steve watched her face cycle through surprise, confusion, and then recognition. Her eyes widened slightly as she took in his appearance, the flamingo shirt and electric blue wig clearly catching her off guard.

"Trevor!" she said, her voice carrying a note of startled laughter. "You scared me. Don't sneak up on me like that."

"Sorry about that, gorgeous," Steve grinned, falling automatically into his performance mode. "Didn't mean to startle you. What are you up to today?"

Stephanie gestured toward the shops around them, her expression relaxing. "My friends are sleeping off hangovers from last night. I'm flying solo today." She paused, studying his face with that same focused attention he remembered from Professor Martinez's economics class. "What about you? Where's your entourage?"

"Group excursion to Atlantis," Steve explained, glancing toward where his friends had disappeared. "Just wanted to say hi first."

"Atlantis, huh?" Stephanie's smile carried a hint of mischief. "That sounds very ... touristy of you."

Before Steve could respond, he heard Derek's voice calling from the direction of the water taxi. "Steve! Come on, man! We're taking off!"

Steve turned to see the water taxi already loaded and pulling away from the dock, his group onboard. Derek was waving from the boat's deck, his gesture somewhere between encouraging and apologetic. The next shuttle wouldn't arrive for another fifteen minutes, and by then, his group would be long gone.

"Looks like your ride left without you," Stephanie observed, her tone carefully neutral.

"We can catch the next one," Steve said quickly, his performance instincts kicking in. "Want to come with? The crew would love to have you join us for the day, and Atlantis is incredible when you go with people who know their way around."

Stephanie tilted her head, studying his face with that same focused attention he remembered from college. "Or," she said, her voice carrying a hint of mischief, "we could stay here. Explore Nassau together. No performance necessary."

Steve sensed a crack inside him. The performance armor he'd carried for nine years now pressed tighter, more suffocating.

"You know what?" he said, his voice losing some of its theatrical projection. "That sounds perfect."

Stephanie's smile was answer enough.

They left the pier shops behind and stepped into Nassau itself, the city breathing past the tourist gloss. Narrower streets, weathered buildings, vendors who wanted to talk rather than sell. Steve's walk softened, his swagger giving way to an easier pace.

"So," Stephanie said as they paused outside a small art gallery, "is this what you do? Cruise around being fabulous?"

"Something like that," Steve replied, but his tone had lost its performative edge. "What about you? Still practicing law?"

"Just finished a very messy divorce," she said, examining a display of local paintings. "Hence the girls' trip. Rachel thought I needed to 're-claim my joy.'" She made air quotes around the phrase, her expression wryly amused.

"And are you? Reclaiming it?"

"Getting there." She turned to face him, and Steve felt the full weight of her attention. "It's strange, you know? Starting over at forty-two. Figuring out who you are when you're not half of a couple anymore."

Steve's chest tightened. "Yeah. I can imagine."

They walked on, steady despite the crush of tourists from seven ships. Stephanie slipped through the crowd with practiced grace, pausing not for trinkets but for the crafts that carried artistry. She wanted to know the techniques, the materials, the stories etched into every piece.

"You're really interested in this stuff," Steve observed as she examined a hand-carved wooden bowl, running her fingers along the smooth surface.

"I love seeing how people create things," she said, then looked at him with a teasing smile. "Remember when you tried to convince me that urban planning was a creative field?"

"It is!" Steve protested, then caught himself. The response had come from somewhere deeper than his usual performance, somewhere that remembered late-night conversations about designing cities that actually worked for people.

"There he is," Stephanie said softly, her eyes lighting up. "I wondered if he was still in there."

Steve was exposed, as if she'd seen through his costume to a part of him he'd long forgotten. "I don't know what you mean."

"Sure you do." She purchased the wooden bowl, chatting easily with the vendor about the local wood used in its construction. "You used to get that exact same look when you talked about architecture. Like you were seeing blueprints in your head."

They moved deeper into the city, past the colonial buildings and into neighborhoods where locals actually lived. Steve's knowledge spilled out as he pointed to architectural details, explaining how different building styles had evolved to handle Caribbean weather. His voice dropped its theatrical projection, becoming more conversational, more real.

"You know," Stephanie said as they paused outside a small church, "I'm starting to think Steve might be the performance, not the other way around."

The observation hit Steve like a physical blow. "What do you mean?"

"Nothing bad," she said quickly, seeing his expression. "Just ... you seem more comfortable when you're not trying to entertain me. Like you can actually breathe."

Steve wanted to argue, to defend the persona that had served him so well for nine years. Instead, he nodded. "Sometimes I forget there's a difference."

"Between what?"

"Between being Steve and being ... myself."

Stephanie stepped closer, her voice gentle. "What if they're both you?"

The question hung in the air between them as they walked toward Senor Frogs, the familiar restaurant chain offering a refuge from the intense Caribbean sun. The place was packed with cruise passengers, the atmosphere boisterous and cheerful. They found a table on the covered patio, close enough to the water to catch the breeze but far enough from the main crowd to have a conversation.

"Two piña coladas," Steve told the server, then caught himself. "Actually, make mine a beer. Something local."

"Kalik," the server suggested with a grin. "Best beer in the Bahamas."

"Perfect." Steve eased back, tension slipping free. "So. Messy divorce. Want to talk about it?"

"Not particularly," Stephanie said, but her tone was amused rather than defensive. "What about you? What's your story? Last time we talked, you were going to change the world through better city planning."

"That was a long time ago," Steve deflected, but Stephanie's steady gaze made it clear she wasn't accepting the brush-off.

"Not that long. Twenty-something years isn't a lifetime."

"Feels like it sometimes."

heir drinks arrived, and Steve took a long swallow of his beer, delaying. The performance he wore so easily felt ill-fitting across from the woman who knew him before Steve, who remembered Trevor.

"You want to know what happened to the guy who was going to change the world?" he asked finally.

"I do."

"He got boring." The words came out more bitter than he'd intended. "Got a job at a warehouse in Dayton. Stocks shelves, manages inventory. Goes home to an empty apartment and watches Netflix until he falls asleep on the couch."

Stephanie's expression didn't change, but her eyes softened. "That doesn't sound boring. That sounds like life."

"Life sucks," Steve said, then caught himself. The bitterness in his voice belonged to Trevor, not Steve. Steve was supposed to be relentlessly positive, infectiously cheerful. "I mean—"

"No, don't." Stephanie leaned forward. "Don't put the costume back on. I like this version better."

"This version is why I created Steve in the first place." The truth slipped free. "Nine years ago, I took a cruise to forget a failed relationship. I was weary of being Trevor Dean Barnes, warehouse supervisor from Ohio, so I chose to be someone different for a week."

"And Steve was born," she added.

"Steve was born." He took another sip of his beer, surprised by how easy it was to talk about this with her. "People loved him. He was fun, charismatic, the life of the party. Everything Trevor wasn't."

"So you kept him."

"I kept him. Started taking more cruises, perfecting the persona. I've got it down to a science now. Color-coded spreadsheets for costume rotations, backup wigs, enough glitter to make a Vegas showgirl jealous." He laughed, but it came out hollow. "Sometimes I think about just being Trevor for a day, but then I remember why I created Steve in the first place."

"Which was?"

"Because Trevor is boring. Trevor doesn't make people happy. Trevor just ... exists."

Stephanie was quiet for a long moment, studying his face. When she spoke, her voice was gentle but firm. "You know what I think?"

"What?"

"I think you're doing both right now. Being Trevor in Steve's clothes." She gestured toward his flamingo shirt and electric blue wig. "And it's working. You're not performing for me anymore. You're just talking. And I like it."

Trevor felt himself fracture. "Even dressed like the Elysian's glitter-drenched court jester?"

"Especially then." Her expression warmed. "It's like you're fearless about being yourself, no matter the costume."

"I'm not brave," Trevor said, and realized he'd stopped thinking of himself as Steve somewhere during the conversation. "I'm terrified. What if Trevor isn't enough? What if people only like the performance?"

"Then they're not your people," Stephanie said simply. "But I don't think that's true. I think you've been Steve for so long, you've forgotten that Trevor was worth knowing too."

"Was he?" Trevor asked, his voice smaller than he'd intended.

"He was." Stephanie reached across the table and touched his hand. "He was curious about the world. He cared about making things better. He made me laugh without trying to be funny. He was … real."

Trevor stared at their joined hands, his flamingo shirt suddenly feeling less like a costume and more like just clothes. "I haven't been real in a long time."

"You're being real now."

"Now I'm scared."

"Good," Stephanie said, her thumb tracing across his knuckles. "That means it matters."

They lingered in quiet, the din of the restaurant softening into background hum. For the first time in years, Trevor breathed without effort, existing without the need to perform.

"Can I ask you something?" he said finally.

"Shoot."

"Why didn't you say anything on the ship?"

Stephanie's smile was soft, nostalgic. "Because I could see you were having fun. And because …" She paused, seeming to choose her words carefully. "Because I wanted to see who you'd become. All of you. Steve and Trevor."

"And what's the verdict?"

"I think they're both you," she said. "And I think you're more interesting than you give yourself credit for. Even in Ohio. Even stocking shelves."

Trevor laughed, and it came out genuine this time. "You always were good at seeing things differently."

"It's a gift," she said with mock solemnity, then grinned. "Plus, I had a lot of practice with you in college. You were always your own worst critic."

"Some things never change."

"Some things shouldn't." She squeezed his hand. "But some things should. Like maybe ... giving yourself permission to be both? Steve and Trevor? Not choosing one or the other?"

Trevor considered this as he finished his beer. The idea felt revolutionary and terrifying at the same time. "I don't know if I remember how to be Trevor around other people."

"You're being Trevor around me right now."

"You're different."

"How?"

"You knew me before." The words came out quietly, like a confession. "You remember when I was just ... me."

"I remember when you were always you," Stephanie corrected gently. "The Trevor I knew in college wasn't boring. He was thoughtful and kind, and he cared about things. That's not boring, that's rare."

Trevor felt tears prick at his eyes and blinked them away. "I really missed you," he said, the words slipping out before he could stop them.

"I missed you, too," Stephanie said. "More than I probably should have, considering I was married to someone else for most of it."

"Are you okay? With the divorce, I mean."

"I'm getting there," she said, then smiled. "This helps. Talking to you. Remembering that there's a world beyond the mess I just left behind."

"And I'm part of that world?"

"If you want to be."

Trevor registered a shift within, as if a door he'd kept barred finally budged. "I want to be. I just ... I don't know how to carry both—Steve and Trevor. I don't know if they belong together."

"Maybe that's something we can figure out together," Stephanie said. "I mean, if you want to. No pressure."

Trevor studied her, recognizing the girl from his past yet struck by the woman she had grown into. She was strong, confident, and present in a way that filled him with a longing he thought he had lost forever.

"I'd like that," he said.

"Good." She signaled the server for the check. "Because I have a feeling Trevor's going to need some practice being himself again."

"And if I mess it up?"

"Then we'll figure it out as we go," Stephanie said. "That's what friends do."

"Friends," Trevor repeated, the word carrying hope instead of resignation.

They left the restaurant and walked back toward the pier, the afternoon sun warm on their faces. Trevor moved differently now, inhabiting his own skin with new ease. The flamingo shirt and electric blue wig were still there, but they felt less like armor and more like … clothes. Ridiculous clothes, maybe, but just clothes.

"So," Stephanie said as they approached the pier shops, "what happens now? Do you turn back into Steve when we get to the ship?"

"I don't know," Trevor admitted. "I haven't thought that far ahead."

"Well," she said, bumping his shoulder with hers, "you don't have to figure it out all at once. Maybe just … see what happens."

"See what happens," Trevor repeated, testing the words. "I like that."

"Good," Stephanie said. "Because I have a feeling this is just the beginning."

As they returned to the ship, Trevor felt a long-buried ember glow within him: hope. Not Steve's manic optimism, but a calmer hope, steady and sure, the kind born of a man no longer fleeing from himself.

Five

The Captain's Haven practically vibrated with competitive energy. Grown adults were already behaving like caffeinated teenagers, and the games hadn't even started. Steve adjusted his simple white T-shirt and mint green shorts, a surprisingly understated look that somehow matched his distracted mood. His electric blue wig stayed perfectly in place, the one constant of his Steve persona. He took in the maritime chaos: fake parrots perched everywhere, a massive treasure chest commanding center stage, and enough nautical props to outfit a theme park.

"Ahoy, me hearties!"

Steve spun around to see Maude making her grand entrance, complete with a tricorn hat, eye patch, and what appeared to be a stuffed parrot duct-taped to her shoulder. She brandished a rolled-up treasure map like she was about to lead a mutiny.

"Prepare for the most legendary treasure hunt on the high seas!" Maude announced, her voice carrying the theatrical flair of someone who'd clearly been practicing her pirate accent in the mirror. "Today, ye scurvy dogs will battle for glory, honor, and the most coveted prize in all the seven seas!"

"What's the prize?" Derek called out, already striking poses with Mike like they were preparing for their victory photos.

Maude grinned wickedly. "The winners become Captain for a day, complete with dining privileges at the Captain's Table and a custom portrait painted by our ship's artist!"

The room erupted in competitive war cries. Nancy immediately started stretching like she was preparing for the Olympics, while Tony cracked his knuckles with the intensity of someone who'd been waiting his entire life for this moment.

"Teams of three!" Maude continued, waving her map dramatically. "And remember, me hearties: the greatest treasures are often found where ye least expect them!"

The performance clicked on like stage lights. "Alright, beautiful people!" Steve called out, his voice carrying that familiar sparkle. "Time to show these amateurs how it's done!"

Cami sauntered over, her statement earrings catching the light as she grinned. "Team Fabulous?" she suggested.

"Obviously," Lila added, appearing beside them with her coral-and-teal hair looking particularly vibrant under the pub's warm lighting. "Though I should warn you, I'm in an exceptionally good mood today."

"Why?" Steve asked, though his attention seemed to drift slightly as he spoke.

"Let's just say last night was ... invigorating," Lila said with a wicked grin.

Steve nodded absently, his eyes scanning the room but clearly not focused on anything in particular. "Mm-hmm. That's ... great."

Cami and Lila exchanged a look. Steve usually demanded details about everything, especially Lila's romantic adventures.

"Behold!" Maude thrust the treasure map toward them with dramatic flair. "Your first challenge awaits in the Celestial Dining Room, but ye must don the proper attire!" She gestured toward a pile of chef's hats and aprons. "For how can ye cook up victory without looking the part?"

Steve automatically grabbed the supplies, but instead of his usual theatrical commentary about the ridiculous costume requirements, he just stared at the chef's hat like it held the secrets of the universe.

"Earth to Steve," Cami said, snapping her fingers. "You're supposed to put it on your head, not commune with it spiritually."

"Right. Yes. Chef hat." Steve mechanically placed it on his head, slightly askew. "Very ... chef-like."

Lila raised an eyebrow. "Okay, that was weird. You usually have at least seventeen jokes about costume requirements."

"I'm focused," Steve said, but his voice lacked its usual conviction. "Strategic thinking. Very important for ... treasure ... hunting."

"Right," Cami said slowly. "Well, let's go dominate this thing before Nancy's team gets too much of a head start."

They joined the stampede toward the door as teams scattered throughout the ship like released zoo animals. The Golden Girls were already power-walking toward the elevators with military precision, while The Fierce Queens had somehow acquired a feather boa and were using it as a team banner.

"This is going to be a bloodbath," Lila observed with obvious delight.

"The best kind," Cami agreed.

Steve nodded along, but his mind seemed to be somewhere else entirely, somewhere that involved dark hair, intelligent brown eyes, and the memory of authentic conversation over local crafts in Nassau's markets.

The Celestial Dining Room had been transformed into what could only be described as maritime trivia chaos. Teams huddled around tables covered with puzzle pieces, historical documents, and what appeared to be scale models of famous cruise ships.

"Your challenge!" announced a crew member dressed as a ship's cook. "Solve the cruise ship history puzzle while wearing your chef attire! First team to complete the timeline wins the next clue!"

Steve's muscle memory kicked in immediately. Cruise ship trivia was his domain, his specialty, his—

"Steve?" Cami waved a hand in front of his face. "You just recited the entire founding history of Carnival Cruise Lines like you were reading a grocery list. While staring dreamily at the ceiling."

"What?" Steve blinked, realizing he'd somehow completed their puzzle without any conscious thought. "Oh. Right. I was ... concentrating."

"You were smiling like you were thinking about puppies," Lila said suspiciously. "Or something else entirely."

"Puppies are great," Steve said weakly, accepting their next clue from the bemused crew member. "Very ... fluffy."

The Topaz Lounge had been converted into what could generously be called organized chaos. Teams were scattered around the elegant space, frantically acting out charades-style clues while other passengers watched from the bar with obvious entertainment.

"Maritime activities!" the challenge coordinator announced. "Act out the cruise ship activity on your card, and your teammates must guess correctly to earn your next clue!"

Steve drew their card and stared at it for a full thirty seconds.

"Shuffleboard," the card read in large, bold letters.

"Okay, easy one," Cami said expectantly. "Go for it."

Steve continued staring at the card like it was written in ancient hieroglyphics.

"Steve?" Lila prompted. "You're supposed to be miming, not having an existential crisis."

"Right. Shuffleboard." Steve looked up and broke into a parody of interpretive dance. The word itself stirred an old memory—Shuffleboard. The senior center. That Saturday afternoon he'd roped Stephanie into joining him for his community service hours, convinced she would hate every second.

Instead, she'd gravitated toward Harold, the eighty-three-year-old widower who'd been sitting alone by the shuffleboard court, watching other residents play with the kind of longing that made your chest ache.

"Mind if I join you, handsome?" she'd asked, settling beside him with that easy smile.

Harold had blushed like a teenager. "I don't know, sweetheart. These old hands aren't what they used to be."

"Good thing I'm terrible at this," she'd laughed, picking up a disc. "We can be awful together."

What followed was the most elaborate flirtation Trevor had ever witnessed. Stephanie asking Harold to "show her proper form," letting him guide her hands while she giggled at his increasingly confident jokes. She'd gasped dramatically at his shots, celebrated his wins, and somehow made losing to him feel like the greatest honor of her life.

"You've still got it, Harold," she'd said, squeezing his arm as he beamed with pride.

Later, the activity coordinator had pulled them aside. "I don't know what you did, but Harold hasn't smiled like that since his wife passed three years ago. He's been asking when you're coming back."

Trevor had watched Stephanie's eyes fill with tears, watched her excuse herself to the bathroom, and realized he was completely, helplessly in love with her kindness.

Somewhere in the distance, he was aware of Cami and Lila's voices, of moving through the ship, but the memory held him like warm water. Stephanie's genuine laugh with Harold, the way she'd made a lonely old man feel young again, the way she'd cared about a stranger's heart just because it was—

THUNK.

Steve's face met the glass poolside door with a sound that reverberated across the entire pool area.

"Oh my God," Cami gasped as Steve stumbled backward, completely dazed.

"Steve!" Lila reached for him, but he was already wobbling, blinking in confusion.

"I'm fine," Steve mumbled, suddenly realizing he was wearing a plastic flower crown and had no memory of how he'd gotten to

Aphrodite's Pool. Had they finished the shuffleboard challenge? The art gallery? His mind scrambled to piece together the last hour.

He backed into a decorative palm tree, which triggered some kind of sensor that activated the pool's elaborate fountain system.

Water erupted in graceful arcs around the pool as Steve stood there, completely soaked in his white T-shirt and mint green shorts, his plastic flower crown now drooping sadly, blinking in confusion while other teams stared in horror.

"Stephen!" Cami's voice reached a pitch that could shatter glass. "What the hell is wrong with you?!"

"Either you're having a stroke or someone has scrambled your brain," Lila assessed, pulling him away from the still-fountaining water feature.

"The ... the sun got in my eyes?" Steve offered weakly, water dripping from his blue wig.

Derek was openly filming with his phone while Nancy pointed and cackled with undisguised glee.

Between challenges, Cami and Lila cornered Steve in a quiet corridor. He was still dripping, still disheveled, and still wearing his soggy flower crown.

"Okay, intervention time," Cami announced. "So that blonde from the piano bar last night seemed nice," she said to Lila, clearly trying to get Steve's attention.

"Rachel. And yes, very nice. Very ... flexible," Lila replied with her usual wicked grin.

"Girl, you're terrible. What happened to taking things slow?"

"Slow is boring. Besides, it was just a one-night thing anyway."

Steve stood there dripping, staring at the ceiling like it held the secrets of the universe.

Cami snapped her fingers in front of his face. "Earth to Steve! Houston, we have a problem!"

Steve startled so violently that he dropped their puzzle clues, which scattered across the corridor floor. "What? Sorry, were you saying something about ... boats?"

"That's it," Lila said dramatically. "You are *gone*. Like, gone-gone. What happened yesterday?"

"Just ... focused on maritime history?" Steve tried.

"That's not focus, that's a fugue state!" Cami declared.

The Ship's Art Gallery had been converted into the final challenge location, with easels and art supplies scattered throughout the elegant space. Teams were attempting to recreate famous paintings using provided props, and the results were ... abstract.

"Your challenge," the coordinator announced, "recreate 'The Scream' using only the materials provided!"

Steve picked up a paintbrush and immediately began creating what could only be described as a wistful landscape. While his teammates stared in disbelief, he painted gentle rolling hills under a peaceful sunset.

"Steve," Lila said carefully, "that's not 'The Scream.' That's more like 'Pleasant Afternoon in Tuscany.'"

"What?" Steve looked at his canvas, seeming surprised by what he'd created.

"Okay, seriously, what's going on with you?" Lila confronted him directly. "You're acting like someone who left half their brain in port."

Steve tried to brush off her observation with jazz hands, but accidentally knocked over the entire easel setup. Paint flew everywhere as the wooden frame clattered to the floor.

"Don't Steve me right now," Lila said firmly as he tried to clean up the mess. "I know distracted when I see it, and honey, you are GONE."

Meanwhile, Tony's team raced past them, having somehow created a masterpiece interpretation of "Dogs Playing Poker" using pool noodles and fake mustaches.

"We're going to lose to septuagenarians," Cami observed with horror.

The teams stumbled back into Captain's Haven in various states of dishevelment. Nancy's team was somehow victorious despite being the oldest, and Nancy was celebrating with what could only be described as inappropriate twerking while wearing a treasure chest costume.

Derek collapsed on the floor like he'd died in a Shakespeare tragedy. "I have been *defeated* by senior citizens!"

"The Golden Girls have claimed victory!" Maude announced, still in full pirate regalia. "But what we witnessed today was ... unprecedented maritime confusion!"

Everyone turned to stare at Steve, who was still damp, still wearing his wilted flower crown, and still looked like he'd been hit by a truck.

"Son," Tony said gently, "I've seen people have midlife crises, but that was something else."

"Steve, are you okay?" Jessica asked innocently. "You looked like you were seeing ghosts."

Steve felt the weight of everyone's attention and realized how completely obvious his distraction had been. His cheeks burned with embarrassment.

Maude cornered him while the others celebrated Nancy's victory.

"Arrr, matey," she said, still maintaining her pirate persona, "sometimes the most important treasure isn't the one you're hunting for."

"Maude, what are you talking about? And why are you still talking like a pirate?"

Maude dropped her character slightly, her voice becoming gentler. "The heart knows when it's found something worth sharing, Steve."

Steve stared at her, finally understanding that he'd been completely transparent all morning.

"Perhaps tomorrow's adventure calls for a different kind of courage," Maude added cryptically before wandering off to congratulate Nancy on her victory.

As the realization struck, Steve felt a lock turn inside him. He had been distracted all morning because part of him wanted Stephanie to see this world he had built. The friendships, the wild energy, the sheer ridiculous fun of it all.

"So," Cami said, settling beside him as the crowd began to thin out, "want to tell us what that was really about?"

"Yeah," Lila added, plopping down on his other side. "Because whatever happened yesterday clearly scrambled your brain in a very specific way."

Steve looked at his teammates. These women who'd just spent two hours watching him malfunction spectacularly and were still here, still concerned, still his friends despite his epic failure.

"I think," he said slowly, "I've been living in separate worlds for too long."

"What do you mean?" Cami asked.

"Nothing," Steve said, shaking his head with a rueful smile. "Just … thinking out loud."

Derek looked up from his dramatic floor position. "Well, whatever it was, it was the most entertaining disaster I've witnessed in years. Tony literally filmed your fountain incident."

"Great," Steve muttered, but he was grinning now. "Just what I needed for posterity."

"Come on," Lila said, standing and offering him a hand up. "Let's get you some lunch before you walk into any more glass doors."

Six

Shimmering heat, the salt-laced breeze, and the hum of Caribbean rhythms drifted through the air of Grand Turk like a welcome banner as Steve and his crew exited the ship. His bright tropical shirt featuring oversized hibiscus flowers in electric pink and orange seemed designed for this exact moment, while the flame-patterned swim trunks underneath were ready for pool action. Even the humidity couldn't touch his perfectly styled electric blue wig.

Just beyond the pier, past the shops bursting with sun hats and rum cake samples, the port opened up into a pastel-colored playground of beach bars, palm trees, and lazy island time. And anchoring the scene was their destination: Margaritaville, where the air smelled like sunscreen and frozen drinks.

"Alright, beautiful people," Steve announced, gesturing grandly toward the elevated cabanas painted in island hues. "I've secured us the VIP treatment. Private cabana, dedicated service, and front-row seats to paradise."

The pool stretched out like a turquoise lagoon, its surface scattered with floats and sun-drenched cruisers cradling daiquiris. The swim-up bar throbbed with music, every beat keeping time with splashes and laughter. It was loud, carefree, a tide of pure revelry.

The Mingle crew followed in his wake like a colorful parade. Derek and Mike wore matching souvenir tees they picked up from the gift shop on the ship, while Cami had chosen a stunning one-piece in deep emerald that made her statement earrings pop. Lila's short coral-and-teal hair caught the sunlight like a prism, and she'd paired a vintage band T-shirt with high-waisted bikini bottoms that showed off her tattooed arms.

"Steve, honey, you've outdone yourself," Tony said, settling into one of the plush loungers with a grateful sigh. At seventy, he moved with the careful precision of someone who'd learned to pace himself, but his eyes sparkled with the same enthusiasm that had made him a Mingle regular for three years running.

"This is what happens when you sail with a legend," Derek declared, already flagging down their server. "Steve doesn't just do vacations, he curates experiences."

Steve felt that familiar warm glow of being exactly who everyone needed him to be, but something was different today. The performance felt lighter somehow, less desperate. Maybe it was the Nassau conversation still echoing in his mind, or maybe it was the way Stephanie had looked at him yesterday when she'd said his name.

"Speaking of experiences," Lila said, stretching out on her lounger like a cat in the sun, "I could get used to this level of luxury. My broke artist budget usually limits me to whatever free beach I can find."

"That's what we're here for," Steve replied, and for once the words felt genuine rather than performative. "Making sure everyone gets to live a little."

Jessica, the newest addition to their group, looked around with wide eyes. "I still can't believe you all do this regularly. It's like being part of some exclusive club."

"The most exclusive," Mike said with a grin. "Membership requires a high tolerance for public embarrassment and an appreciation for tropical drinks before noon."

"And an ability to keep up with Steve's energy," Cami added, though her tone was affectionate. "Speaking of which, what's the plan, ringmaster?"

Steve was about to launch into his usual elaborate activity coordination when he spotted them across the pool area. Stephanie and her friends had claimed a spot near the main bar, their laughter carrying across the water as Becca told what appeared to be a very animated story.

For a moment, Steve lingered on her. The sundress, the wind in her hair, the ease in her bearing—it all struck him at once. She looked unburdened, so at home in her own skin that he ached with a longing he hadn't expected.

"Steve?" Lila's voice cut through his reverie. "You're doing that thing again."

"What thing?"

"That dreamy, far-away look. Like you're watching something the rest of us can't see."

Steve felt heat creep up his neck. "I was just ... surveying the area. Strategic planning."

"Uh-huh," Cami said, following his gaze. "Strategic planning. Is that what we're calling it?"

Before Steve could deflect, Tony surprised everyone by chuckling. "Son, I've been married forty-seven years. I know that look. And it's not strategy."

"Tony's right," Derek said, sitting up with obvious interest. "That's the look of a man who's spotted something worth investigating."

Steve's shoulders tensed under their collective attention, but instead of his usual manic deflection, he laughed. Really laughed, in a way that came from somewhere deeper than his performance persona.

"You are all impossible," he said, shaking his head. "Can't a guy appreciate beautiful scenery without getting the third degree?"

"Not when the guy is Steve and the scenery involves people," Lila replied with a wicked grin. "Come on, spill. Who caught your eye?"

And that's when Steve made a decision that surprised everyone, including himself.

"Actually," he said, his grin shifting into full performance mode, "I think it's time to expand our little paradise."

Without another word, Steve dove into the pool with theatrical flair, his hibiscus shirt billowing as he hit the water. He swam across the turquoise expanse with confident strokes, his electric blue wig somehow staying perfectly in place, drawing attention from other guests lounging poolside.

He surfaced at the swim-up bar where Stephanie and her friends were perched on submerged stools, tropical drinks in hand, the warm Caribbean water lapping at their waists.

"Ladies!" Steve called out, his trademark sparkle undimmed as water streamed from his wig, a little mussed but impressively still in place. "I come bearing an invitation you cannot refuse!"

"Steve!" Stephanie laughed, clearly delighted by his dramatic entrance. "Only you would make a pool crossing look like a Broadway number."

"Please tell me you're here to save us from this philosophical debate about whether piña coladas count as breakfast," Becca said, gesturing to their drinks.

"They absolutely count as breakfast," Steve declared with authority, "but I come bearing an upgrade. VIP cabana, full service, and pool games so epic Margaritaville will be telling stories for years."

"Say no more," Rachel said immediately. "We were just commenting on how we needed more chaos in our day."

Steve's grin widened to megawatt intensity. "Chaos is my specialty, gorgeous. Plus, my crew has been dying to hang out with you again."

"The famous Mingle crew!" Angela said warmly. "I was hoping we'd run into you today."

"Follow me, beautiful people," Steve said, pushing off from the swim-up bar with a characteristic flourish. "Time to show this resort how VIP relaxation is really done."

As they crossed the pool area toward his cabana, Steve felt that familiar buzz of being the linchpin, the one who made it all flow. With both groups already meshing, he could shift into his favorite gear—shaping the perfect vacation experience.

Within minutes of reaching the premium cabana area, Steve had everyone settled with fresh drinks and perfectly positioned loungers. He moved between the groups with effortless grace, making sure Angela had the shade she preferred, flagging down their server for Becca's specific cocktail request, and ensuring Tony had easy access to the cooler without having to get up from his comfortable spot.

"Look at him go," Derek murmured to Stephanie as they watched Steve coordinate everything with the precision of a cruise director. "Nine years of this, and he still acts like everyone's comfort is his personal mission."

"You haven't seen anything yet," Tony said with obvious affection, accepting the cold beer Steve had just handed him without being asked. "This one's got enough energy to power a small city. But he's got a good heart underneath all the sparkle."

"The best heart," Lila added.

"Alright, enough roasting the host," Steve declared, but he was grinning. "Who's ready for some pool games?"

Within minutes, he had everyone organized for floating beer pong using pool noodles and plastic cups. Steve thrived on elaborate setups like this, his genius for turning a simple pool into an arena for competitive fun.

"Partners?" he asked, looking around the group.

"I'll take Steve," Stephanie said without hesitation, moving to stand beside him. As she leaned in to help arrange the makeshift playing field, she lowered her voice so only he could hear. "Are you still the pong master from college? You always knew how to get people to have fun."

"I might still have a few tricks up my sleeve," he managed with a grin.

The game unfolded in a blur of playful uproar. Derek and Mike revealed a fierce competitive streak, Becca's trash talk drew cheers,

Angela astonished with pinpoint aim, and Rachel's commentary left the whole group howling. Steve's laughter spilled out unforced as he caught Stephanie ribbing Derek about his rainbow tank top while Angela leaned closer to hear one of Tony's stories about his late wife.

It felt effortless. Not just being with Stephanie, but the way everyone moved around each other, conversations flowed and overlapped without anyone working to make it happen. Steve realized he'd stopped orchestrating and started simply existing.

"This is perfect," Stephanie said, watching Derek attempt to teach Angela a volleyball move that created more splashing than points. "They're a riot."

"They are," Steve agreed, grinning. "I've been sailing with some of them for years, but today ... I don't know. It feels different."

"Different how?"

"Like I don't have to keep the party afloat. They make it happen on their own."

Stephanie turned to study his profile, noting the way the late afternoon light caught the blue in his wig but also highlighted the contentment in his expression. "That's what happens when you stop performing and start just being present."

Her words landed with startling clarity, cutting through everything, straight to the truth he'd been avoiding. The integration had been effortless—friend groups blending, laughter shared, natural connections forming everywhere he looked.

"Hey," he said, turning to face her fully. "I know we're all supposed to head back soon, but ..." He paused, suddenly nervous in a way that had nothing to do with performance anxiety. "Would you be interested in spending some time together tonight? Just the two of us?"

Stephanie's smile was immediate and warm. "I was hoping you'd ask."

"Yeah?" Steve felt that recognizable flutter of excitement, but this time it came from somewhere deeper than his usual performance high. "I could show you some of the quieter parts of the ship. Places where we could actually talk without an audience."

"That sounds perfect." She leaned closer, lowering her voice. "I have to admit, as much as I love your cruise family, I've been wanting some time to get to know you better. The real you."

The words should have terrified him. Instead, a quiet certainty anchored inside him, the sense of finally belonging.

"The real me might surprise you," he said, his voice softer than his usual Steve projection.

"I'm counting on it."

From across the pool, Lila called out, "Alright, love birds, we're starting to migrate back to the ship if you want to catch the next tender!"

Steve laughed, the sound unforced. "Duty calls," he said, standing and offering Stephanie his hand. "But tonight?"

"Tonight," she confirmed, letting him pull her up from the pool's edge.

As they joined the rest of the group for the walk back to the pier, Steve wove naturally between the two groups of friends, no longer feeling like he was performing for anyone but simply existing as himself. Whatever that meant.

"So," Cami said, falling into step beside him as they made their way down the pier, "college, huh?"

Steve's step faltered slightly. "What?"

"I happened to overhear Stephanie mention college during that beer pong setup. 'Back in college,' she said." Cami's tone was curious, not accusatory. "Funny thing is, you told us you just met her a few days ago."

Steve tried to deflect with a laugh. "People say things like that all the time."

But Cami didn't let it go. Her expression was kind but determined. "Steve, honey, I've seen you charm strangers. This is different. The way you two move together, the way you finish each other's sentences ... that's not new chemistry, that's history."

The words hit Steve with unexpected force. He looked around at his chosen family, the elaborate network of friendships he'd spent nine years creating, and realized how transparent he'd been.

"How long have you actually known her?" Cami asked gently.

"It's ... complicated," Steve said finally.

"Most good things are." Cami smiled knowingly, her expression suggesting she'd been waiting for this conversation all along. "Just know that whatever the story is, I'm glad you found each other ... again."

Seven

T he Topaz Lounge sparkled in the early evening light, crystal chandeliers casting warm patterns across jewel-toned velvet seating. Steve adjusted his deep teal button-down and checked his watch for the third time in five minutes.

"You're making me nervous just watching you," Lila said, swirling her martini with practiced elegance. Her hair was styled in soft waves tonight, and she'd traded her usual band T-shirts for a sleek black dress that showed off her tattooed arms. "I take it your dinner with Stephanie is tonight?"

"I'm not nervous," Steve protested, then immediately contradicted himself by checking his watch again. "I'm just ... punctual."

"Uh-huh." Cami leaned back in her chair, her statement earrings catching the light as she studied Steve with obvious amusement. She looked stunning in emerald silk that complemented her rich skin tone, every inch the successful professional relaxing after a perfect day. "And I suppose that's why you've rearranged your shirt collar four times since we sat down?"

Steve's hand froze halfway to his collar. "I was just—"

"Making sure you look perfect for your romantic dinner," Lila finished with a wicked grin. "After watching you two at Margaritaville today, I'm surprised it took this long for you to ask her out properly."

Steve laughed, feeling caught but oddly okay with it. With these two women, he'd relaxed over the past few days, letting some of his natural personality show through the Steve persona. "You're both impossible."

"We're observant," Cami teased. "You two keep orbiting each other. Call it what you want, but we can all see it."

"Speaking of heading somewhere," Lila said, taking a delicate sip of her martini, "I have my own dinner plans tonight. With Rachel, actually."

"Rachel?" Steve raised an eyebrow. "Stephanie's friend?"

"The very same." Lila's grin turned slightly predatory. "I'm looking forward to hearing her ... oral arguments."

Cami nearly choked on her wine. "Jesus, Lila. Do you ever take a break?"

"Life's too short for boring conversations," Lila replied with a shrug. "Besides, she approached me. Said she was looking forward to a thorough examination of her briefs."

Steve's laughter surprised him, emerging from somewhere deeper than his usual performance mode. "And what about you, Cami? Any romantic adventures planned?"

"I'm keeping my options open," Cami said with a mysterious smile. "Sometimes the best company is your own."

Steve was about to respond when he spotted movement near the lounge entrance. Stephanie appeared in the doorway, and his breath caught. She was wearing a deep burgundy dress that seemed to shimmer in the ambient lighting, her dark hair falling in soft waves around her shoulders. She looked elegant and confident, but when her eyes found his across the room, her smile was pure warmth.

"That's her," he said unnecessarily, already standing.

"Go," Lila said with an encouraging wave. "And Steve? Breathe."

"Have fun, honey," Cami added. "And try not to overthink everything."

Steve made his way across the lounge, weaving between other guests enjoying pre-dinner cocktails. As he approached Stephanie, that familiar flutter of excitement came from somewhere deeper than his usual performance high.

"You look incredible," he said.

"Thank you." Her smile lit up her entire face. "You clean up pretty well yourself. I like the more sophisticated Steve."

"Still Steve," he replied with a grin, "just dialed back a few notches for fine dining."

She looked over his shoulder and waved. "I see Lila and Cami are holding down the fort. I should go say hello properly."

"Stephanie!" Lila called out as they approached. "You look absolutely stunning."

"The famous dinner date," Cami added with obvious delight, rising to give Stephanie a quick hug. "I love that dress on you. Very 'I'm about to charm the pants off a certain cruise ship legend.'"

"Thank you both," Stephanie replied laughing at Cami's directness. "You two look incredible yourselves. Girls' night at the Topaz Lounge?"

"Actually, I have my own plans tonight," Lila said with her characteristic confidence. "With your friend Rachel."

"Oh, she mentioned!" Stephanie grinned. "She was practically vibrating with excitement when she left to get ready. I think you made quite an impression."

"I do tend to have that effect," Lila replied with a wicked smile. "Don't worry, I'll take excellent care of her."

"Just don't completely scandalize her," Stephanie laughed. "Rachel's been all work and no play for way too long."

"Scandalize? Me?" Lila gasped with exaggerated innocence. "I'm simply going to provide a thorough education in the finer points of Caribbean nightlife."

"That's exactly what I'm worried about," Stephanie grinned.

"Well, while you two are corrupting lawyers and charming cruise legends," Cami interjected with theatrical drama, "I'll be living my best hermit life. Room service, trashy novel, and absolutely zero romantic complications."

"Look at you, getting all antisocial," Lila teased. "What happened to 'life's too short for boring conversations'?"

"Sometimes life's too short for any conversations at all," Cami shot back with a satisfied smile. "Besides, someone needs to live vicariously through your inevitable disaster stories tomorrow."

"Hey!" Steve protested. "Why does everyone assume I'm going to create disaster stories?"

"Experience," all three women said in unison, then burst into laughter.

Steve absorbed their banter, a long-held tightness giving way. Seeing Stephanie move easily among his chosen family felt like a lock finally giving.

"We should probably head to dinner," he said. "Our reservation is in fifteen minutes."

"Go create some beautiful chaos," Cami said with an encouraging wave.

"And remember," Lila added with a theatrical wink, "if Graham sleeps peacefully tonight, you've failed."

Steve threw back his head and laughed. "You're absolutely terrible," he said, but his grin was pure delight. "Poor Graham doesn't deserve whatever chaos you're imagining."

"That's what makes it fun," Lila replied with satisfaction. "Make him earn that head of security promotion."

As they left the lounge, Steve's movements held ease rather than performance. With Stephanie, his showmanship settled into a grounded charm, threaded with honesty.

"Your friends are great," Stephanie said as they made their way toward Ember & Tide. "I can see why you've been sailing with them for so long."

"They're the best kind of vacation family," Steve replied, surprised by his own honesty. "The kind that sees you at your most relaxed and still chooses to sail with you again."

Stephanie glanced at him with interest. "That sounds like there's a story there."

"Maybe," Steve said with a smile. "I'll tell you over dinner."

The Ember & Tide steakhouse enveloped them in warm, intimate luxury. Rich mahogany walls gleamed under the soft glow of flickering sconces, and the gentle murmur of conversation created the perfect backdrop for romance. Their booth offered privacy without isolation, the leather seating inviting them to settle in and stay awhile.

"This is beautiful," Stephanie said, sliding into the booth across from him. "I feel like I should be wearing pearls and speaking in a Mid-Atlantic accent."

"Please don't," Steve said with a laugh. "I like your actual voice too much."

The server appeared with menus and water, giving them a moment to settle in. Steve studied Stephanie across the table, noting the way the candlelight caught the gold flecks in her brown eyes, the easy confidence in her posture.

"So," she said, leaning forward slightly, "tell me about this chosen family of yours. What kinds of bullshit do they see through?"

Steve grinned, launching into stories that surprised him with their authenticity. "Well, there was the time Cami decided she was going to prove she could out-drink anyone on the ship. She challenged this group of college guys to a tequila contest at El Corazón."

"Oh no." Stephanie laughed. "How did that go?"

"She won, obviously. But the best part was watching her give them a lecture about responsible drinking while she was still perfectly composed and they were barely standing. She made them promise to hydrate and eat something before sending them back to their cabins."

"That sounds like quite a woman." Stephanie leaned closer, her amusement clear. "Taking care of people even while proving her point."

"That's Cami in a nutshell. What about Lila?"

"Lila once got matching tattoos with a guy she'd known for exactly six hours. They met at the midnight buffet, hit it off, and by sunrise, they both had tiny cartoon flamingos wearing sunglasses tattooed on their inner thighs."

"She didn't."

"She absolutely did. I found her the next morning at breakfast, still wearing his T-shirt, showing off her new ink to anyone who'd listen. When I asked if she planned to see him again, she just shrugged and said, 'That's not really the point, is it?'"

"What happened to the guy?"

"Never saw him again after that cruise. But Lila still has the flamingo." Steve chuckled, memory bright in his tone. "She called it the perfect souvenir, a keepsake for a moment that was fleeting by design."

After placing their orders with the server, they leaned back thoughtfully.

"These two have been my anchor through dozens of cruises—Cami keeping me grounded, Lila making sure I never miss the moment. And then, of course, there's Maude, our dysfunctional family's matriarch, who always knows exactly what I need to hear."

"That's actually really sweet," Stephanie said, her expression softening. "It's like you've found your chosen family."

"Exactly. Though their idea of taking care of me involves a lot of unsolicited romantic advice and impromptu interventions in my love life."

Stephanie shook her head in amazement. "It's fascinating how people become different versions of themselves on vacation. Like, I guarantee Cami isn't challenging college kids to drinking contests in her regular life."

"Are you sure?" Steve asked with exaggerated surprise. "You mean most people don't settle everyday disputes with tequila competitions?"

"Shocking, I know." Stephanie grinned, then her expression grew more thoughtful. "You know what's funny? I used to think vacation was just about escaping your real life. But being here ... I think it's more about permission to be yourself."

Her words struck, catching him off guard. "What do you mean?"

"For nine years, I was Kevin's wife, molding myself into whoever he needed me to be. Perfect hostess, agreeable partner, the woman who never made waves." She swept her hand toward the elegant surroundings. "But here, for the first time in forever, I get to just be Stephanie. No one else's expectations to meet."

"That must feel incredible," Steve said quietly.

"It does. Terrifying, but incredible ..." She paused, studying his face with curious eyes. "What about you? You seem so ... natural at this whole cruising thing. Like you were born for it."

The question hit hard. She was discovering who she was, while he had wasted years perfecting a mask.

"I guess I've found my element here," he said carefully. "The energy, the people, the whole experience. It brings out the best in me."

Stephanie reached across the table and touched his hand lightly. "I can see that. You light up when you talk about your cruise family, when you're organizing things, making people happy. It's like watching someone do exactly what they're meant to do."

Their appetizers arrived, giving Steve a moment to process her words. As they settled into their meal, the conversation shifted to safer ground, with both of them people-watching other diners and spinning elaborate backstories for couples at nearby tables.

"The couple by the window," Stephanie said, gesturing subtly. "Tax attorney, yoga instructor. First cruise together."

Steve studied the serious man checking his phone while the woman photographed her salad. "Plot twist: he's been googling 'what is quinoa' all week. She thinks this is a wellness retreat."

"And he booked it for the unlimited Wi-Fi package," Stephanie added, grinning. "She's trying to get him to do couples meditation on the sun deck."

"Meanwhile, she's been sneaking bacon cheeseburgers from room service."

"And he's hiding in the sports bar watching ESPN."

They both started laughing, and nostalgia rolled over Steve. "God, we're really doing the pizza place game again, aren't we?"

"Some habits die hard," Stephanie said, wiping her eyes. "What about those two by the bar?"

Steve followed her gaze to a woman elaborately photographing her cocktail while her date watched adoringly. "Food blogger meets hedge fund guy. She thinks he's authentic, he thinks she'll make him Instagram famous."

"But she's been living on crackers all week because she's seasick," Stephanie jumped in.

"And he's been practicing 'candid' poses in the bathroom mirror."

They dissolved into giggles again, the years collapsing between them.

"You know what I miss about us?" Stephanie said when she could breathe. "This. The way we could turn people-watching into performance art."

Steve's hand instinctively went to his eyebrow, and Stephanie's grin widened.

"You still do that," she said softly, her voice filled with recognition. "That little surprised look when you say something completely genuine."

The knowledge that she remembered such a small detail hit deep, leaving him silent, staring at her across the candlelit table. To be seen as Trevor, not Steve, was as terrifying as it was wonderful.

"I ..." he started, then stopped, his voice rougher than usual. "You really see him, don't you? Even with all this?" He gestured vaguely at his Steve ensemble.

"Especially with all this," she said gently. "The costume doesn't hide you, Trevor. It just makes you braver."

As their meals arrived, Steve sensed a shift between them. Conversation came easily: stories, jokes, and observations about cruise ship absurdities. But under it all, a connection was building, stronger than the playful surface.

As they finished their meal, Stephanie sat back with a satisfied sigh. "That was incredible. And I don't just mean the food."

"Good company makes everything better," Steve agreed, meaning it completely.

"What now?" she asked, her eyes meeting his across the table.

Her voice carried such anticipation that his answer came out rougher than intended. "How do you feel about stargazing?"

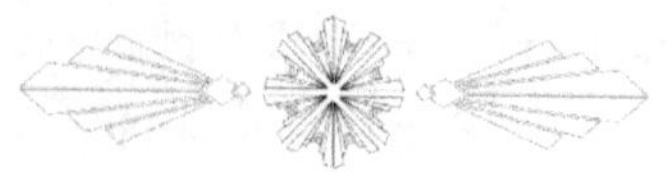

The Celestial View lounge felt like stepping into a dream. The glass-domed ceiling revealed an endless expanse of stars, brilliant points of light scattered across the dark canvas of the Caribbean night. Crescent-shaped loungers were arranged throughout the space, designed for intimate conversation under the cosmos.

Steve led Stephanie to a lounger near the edge of the dome, where they could lie back and lose themselves in the vastness above. The space was nearly empty, with just a few other couples scattered throughout, their quiet conversations creating a gentle murmur that somehow made the night feel more private.

"This is incredible," Stephanie breathed, settling beside him on the plush cushions. "It's like being in our own private planetarium."

"One of my favorite spots on the ship," Steve said, his voice softer now, more intimate. "There's something about being surrounded by all that space that makes everything else feel ... I don't know, more manageable."

They lay back together, shoulders touching, looking up at the star-filled sky. The gentle motion of the ship created a subtle rocking sensation that was oddly comforting.

"You know what I love about travel?" Stephanie said after a few minutes of comfortable silence. "It strips away all the stuff you think defines you. Your job, your routine, your usual roles. And what's left is just ... you."

Steve turned his head to look at her profile, illuminated by the soft ambient lighting. "Is that what this trip has been for you?"

"Definitely. I'm still figuring out who I am when I'm not performing for someone else." She laughed softly. "Turns out I'm the kind of woman who books solo trips and strikes up conversations with mysterious men in pool bars. Who knew?"

"Hey now," Steve said with mock offense, "I wasn't exactly a stranger."

"Fair point." She grinned, then grew more thoughtful. "But that's the thing. I spent so long being who everyone else needed me to be that I forgot who I actually was."

"And now you're figuring it out?"

"Still working on it." She turned to face him, her expression curious in the starlight. "What about you? What are you discovering about yourself out here?"

The question struck deeper than Steve expected. "I think ... cruises draw out the best in me. Here, I turn confident, social, the kind of man who makes things happen. Back home it's different—work, routine, days that blur together without color."

"Which one feels more like you?"

Steve was quiet for a long moment, watching the stars wheel slowly overhead. "This version. The one who can make people laugh, who brings friends together ..." He paused. "I guess I always worried that regular Trevor wasn't interesting enough."

Stephanie's hand found his in the darkness, their fingers intertwining naturally. "I think you're selling Trevor short."

"You don't even know Trevor anymore," he said, but without his usual defensive edge.

"Maybe not. But the way you take care of your friends, the way you make everyone feel included and valued? That doesn't come from a costume, Steve. That's just who you are."

Something cracked open in his chest at her words. He turned fully to face her, studying her expression in the soft light filtering through the dome.

"Why are you really on this cruise, Stephanie?" he asked quietly.

She was silent for a moment, considering. "Because I woke up one day and realized I'd been living someone else's life. When I found out Kevin was cheating, you know what he said when I confronted him? That I was boring. That I never took risks."

"Jesus, Stephanie."

"The worst part was, he wasn't entirely wrong. I'd made myself so small, so safe, that there wasn't much left to discover." She squeezed his hand. "So, I decided to find out who I actually am. And what better way than to spend Kevin's alimony check on a girls' trip to the Caribbean?"

Steve laughed. "I like your style."

"I figured he owed me at least one adventure." Her smile turned wicked. "Though I don't think he had this in mind when he signed the divorce papers."

"And what have you discovered so far?"

"I'm braver than I thought. More curious." She smiled, and in the starlight, she was radiant. "More interested in mysterious men with blue wigs who organize pool parties."

"Mysterious, huh?"

"The most mysterious part is that you don't seem to know how incredible you are."

The words hung in the air between them, heavy with meaning. Steve went completely still as Stephanie shifted closer, her face now just inches from his.

"Stephanie ..." he started, but whatever he'd been planning to say dissolved as she leaned in and kissed him.

The kiss started soft, but within seconds it became hungrier, more urgent. Twenty-two years collapsed into nothing as muscle memory took over. The way she tilted her head, the way he instinctively pulled her closer, the familiar taste that shouldn't have been familiar but somehow was. Stephanie's fingers tangled in his hair, and he dimly registered the synthetic texture of his wig, but it didn't matter. Nothing mattered except the desperate sweetness of this connection, the way their bodies remembered each other despite the decades that had been between them.

When they finally broke apart, both breathing hard, Stephanie kept her hands in his hair, her forehead pressed against his.

"I've been wanting to do that since Nassau," she whispered.

"Why didn't you?" Steve asked, his voice rougher than usual.

"Because I wanted to be sure it was really you who wanted me, not just the performance."

The distinction hit Steve like a gentle punch to the gut. "And now?"

"Now I know." She smiled, her thumb tracing along his cheekbone. "The question is, what do we do about it?"

Steve looked into her eyes, seeing desire and affection. Terror and exhilaration battled for control as he realized what this moment meant.

"Let's get out of here," he said quietly, his voice rough with want.

"Yes," she said without hesitation, her fingers tightening in his hair. "Please."

Steve's stateroom felt impossibly intimate after the vast openness of the stargazing lounge. Soft lighting from the bedside lamps created a warm, golden glow that made everything feel dreamlike.

Stephanie moved to the balcony doors, her hand on the handle as she looked through the glass at the ocean stretching endlessly into the darkness. "Can we …?" she asked, gesturing toward the balcony.

"Of course," Steve said, reaching around her to unlock and slide open the doors.

They stepped outside together, the salt-sweet Caribbean breeze immediately enveloping them. The gentle sound of waves filled the air, and Stephanie moved to the railing, gripping it lightly as she gazed out at the night.

"It's beautiful," she said softly. "Like we're the only two people in the world."

Steve came up behind her, his arms sliding around her waist as he pulled her back against his chest. She melted into him naturally, her hands covering his where they rested against her stomach. "Sometimes it feels that way out here," he murmured against her ear. "Like real life is something that happens to other people."

She leaned into him, her head fitting easily against his shoulder. They swayed with the ship's motion, the night air cool around them. The casual tone of dinner had given way to a silence thick with expectation.

Stephanie turned in his arms so they were face-to-face, her hands sliding up to rest on his chest. "Can I ask you something?"

"Anything," he replied, meaning it.

She looked into his eyes, as if weighing her words. "I want to stay tonight. I want to be with you."

His breath caught. Her touch sent his pulse skittering. "Stephanie …"

"But," she continued, her voice gentle but sure, "I want Trevor."

Eight

Trevor's hands trembled as he reached for the electric blue wig with one hand while pulling Stephanie against him with desperate need. The synthetic hair fell away as their mouths crashed together, chemistry they'd thought long dead roaring back to life in a kiss that tasted of champagne and possibility.

"Trevor," she gasped against his lips, her fingers diving into his real hair. Salt-and-pepper, soft, completely him. The sound of his actual name on her lips made his pulse spike with electric intensity.

Years of practiced defenses fell away in that breathless moment as she saw him without the costume, and she did not turn aside. Instead, she drew nearer, her hands exploring the texture of his real hair with near-reverent care.

They stumbled toward the bed, hands everywhere, fumbling with buttons and fabric, neither willing to break contact long enough to walk properly. Stephanie's fingers worked at his shirt with urgent purpose, nails scraping his chest as she pushed the tropical fabric away from his shoulders.

"Jesus, Steph," he gasped against her throat as she bit down on his collarbone, marking him with her teeth. The sharp sensation made him groan, his hands finding the zipper of her burgundy dress.

"Don't slow down," she breathed against his neck, her voice rough with want.

Performance accessories littered the floor as the last remnants of Steve fell away, rings and chains abandoned for this moment of absolute truth. Her dress slid down her body as his hands mapped every revealed inch, urgent with the need to touch every part of her.

The moonlight streaming through the balcony doors revealed Trevor's authentic form: the slight softness at his waist, the silver threading through his chest hair, real and imperfect and achingly desired.

"God, you're so beautiful," his voice cracked with emotion as he traced the line from her throat to her breast, marveling at the way her skin flushed under his touch.

"You gonna keep chatting or are we gonna fuck?" she said, pulling him down until their bodies aligned, skin to heated skin.

Trevor's breath caught at her directness, heat flooding through him at the raw want in her voice. "Christ, Stephanie," he breathed, any remaining hesitation dissolving completely. His mouth crashed against hers with renewed hunger, all tender exploration replaced by desperate need.

"I've wanted this from the second you walked back into my life," he murmured, voice frayed with need. "Wanted you in ways I can't seem to stop."

"Then stop talking and take me," she replied, her teeth grazing his lower lip before she bit down just hard enough to make him groan.

His hands explored her with reverent hunger, cupping her breasts as his thumbs circled her nipples until she arched with a sharp intake of breath. Her fingernails raked down his back, leaving marks neither wanted to hide. When she guided his hand between her legs, he found her already slick with want, the discovery making his cock throb with anticipation.

"Touch me," she demanded breathlessly, her own fingers wrapping around his hardness, stroking the length of him until he groaned her name like a prayer.

Trevor pulled back from her grip and kissed his way down her body, his tongue circling each nipple before trailing lower. Her stomach muscles jumped under his lips as he moved down, further down, until he was settled between her thighs.

"Trevor," she gasped, her back arching off the bed as his breath ghosted over her slit.

His tongue made the first slow pass, and her hips bucked involuntarily. Her hands flew to his hair, fingers threading through the salt-and-pepper strands as she held him against her.

"Fuck, yes," she breathed, her thighs trembling against his shoulders as he found a rhythm that made her toes curl.

He alternated between broad strokes and focused attention on her clit, her increasingly desperate moans guiding him. Her grip in his hair tightened, her hips rolling against his mouth.

"Trevor, I can't—" she gasped, tugging at his hair. "I need you inside me. Now."

He lifted his head, his lips glistening, and crawled back up her body.

His hands shook as he fumbled for protection, tearing open the condom with clumsy fingers while Stephanie's soft laughter at his haste only made him harder. "Hurry," she whispered, opening her legs to welcome him home as he settled between her thighs, the heat of her core making him ache.

The first touch of his tip against her entrance made them both gasp at the electric contact. He slid against her wetness, coating himself in her arousal, the intimacy of it overwhelming. Her hands gripped his shoulders as he positioned himself, then slowly pushed inside her.

The sensation was devastating. She enveloped him, gripped him, drew him deeper until he was fully seated inside her velvet embrace. They both cried out at the perfection of connection, overwhelmed by how right it felt.

"Fuck," he breathed, fully inside her, their foreheads pressed together as they savored this moment of absolute connection. "You feel incredible."

She tightened her legs around him, adjusting her hips to take him even deeper. "Move," she breathed, her voice shaky with need, hands grasping his ass, urging him on.

They began to move together, his first thrusts slow, withdrawing until just the tip remained inside before driving back into her heat. Each glide sent shockwaves through both of them, but the restraint couldn't last. Stephanie's hips rose to meet him, setting a demanding pace that spoke of years of want finally unleashed.

"You feel so good," Trevor growled, his voice rough as he drove deeper. He angled his hips until she cried out sharply, then held that perfect position, pushing deeper as her nails dug into his back in encouragement.

"Right there," she gasped, her inner walls fluttering around him. "Don't stop."

Her legs locked around his waist, pulling him deeper with each thrust. The wet sounds of their joining filled the air, mixing with her breathless moans and his guttural groans. He could feel her getting wetter, her body opening for him completely as they found their rhythm.

His hand slipped between them, fingers finding her swollen clit. The moment he touched her there, she bucked against him with a strangled cry.

"Oh fuck, yes," she breathed, her head thrown back as he circled that sensitive bundle of nerves while continuing to thrust into her.

The dual sensation was driving her wild. Her body clenched around his cock as he worked her clit with steady pressure, her breathing becoming ragged.

"I'm close," she gasped, every muscle drawn tight beneath him, her nails leaving crescents in his shoulders.

"Me too," he managed, his own control unraveling as she tightened around him like a vice, the pressure building at the base of his spine.

"Don't stop," she cried, her voice breaking as the first waves of her climax began to crash over her.

"Trevor, oh God, Trevor!" She shattered beneath him, her body convulsing as her orgasm tore through her. Her inner walls clamped down around his cock, pulsing and gripping him with devastating intensity, her back arching off the bed as waves of pleasure crashed over her.

The sight and sensation of her coming undone beneath him, the way she cried his real name as she climaxed, pushed him over the edge. He drove deep one final time, his own release exploding through him as he spilled into the condom, her name torn from his throat like a confession of everything he'd been hiding.

They broke together, both undone completely, trembling and gasping, hearts hammering against each other's chests as the aftershocks rippled through them. Trevor collapsed against her, both of them slick with sweat and still breathing hard, neither willing to break the connection between their bodies.

For long moments, they held each other as the waves receded, Trevor still buried inside her, neither willing to break the spell of absolute connection. When he finally had to withdraw to deal with the condom, she pulled him immediately back against her, unwilling to lose the skin-to-skin contact.

When Trevor could finally speak, the words came out wonder-struck.

"That was …"

"I know," Stephanie breathed, understanding perfectly, her fingers tracing his face like she was memorizing him.

"Well, that was definitely the best sex I've had since college," Stephanie said later, her voice lazy and satisfied against his chest.

Trevor's surprised laughter made his whole body shake beneath her. The tension-breaking humor washed away all his anxiety, leaving behind pure contentment instead of performance pressure.

"We were never exactly serious back then," she continued with honest reflection, "but God, the chemistry was always incredible. I used to think about you sometimes … over the years."

"I thought about you, too," Trevor admitted quietly. "More than I probably should have."

Stephanie curled against him, his arm wrapped around her, fingers tracing lazy patterns on her bare shoulder. Her breathing against his ribs gradually slowed from frantic to peaceful as her fingers traced Trevor's form, tracing his collarbone, threading through the sparse hair on his chest.

He watched her touch him with quiet amazement. No performance required, just genuine affection and curiosity. She pressed soft kisses to his sternum, his shoulder, gentle affection that spoke of satisfaction and growing tenderness.

"Your skin is so warm," she whispered. "I love how you feel."

Their legs tangled naturally, bodies fitting together perfectly in the moonlight streaming through the open balcony doors. The sound of waves provided a gentle soundtrack to their quiet discoveries.

After several minutes of comfortable silence, Stephanie's voice cut through the peace with characteristic directness.

"Tell me about him. What atrocity happened to Trevor after college that led to the creation of Steve?"

Trevor's breath caught, then he let out a soft laugh despite himself. "Jesus, Steph. You really don't hold back, do you?"

"Not my strong suit," she admitted, her fingers still tracing circles on his chest. "But I can see it in you. Steve wasn't born from boredom."

She was right, of course. After what they'd just shared, honesty felt not just possible but necessary.

Stephanie's hand moved from tracing circles on his chest to stroking along his collarbone, grounding him for what came next.

Trevor took a shuddering breath, the words feeling like they might tear him apart. "Not too long after college, I met Michelle. Things were good between us, really good. I thought ... I thought everything might work out."

His voice was already rougher, the memory tugging at a depth he rarely touched. Stephanie's fingers moved to his neck, gentle and soothing.

"Then about thirteen years ago, my mom got sick. Cancer." The word came out broken. "I became her primary caregiver. Spent years ... God, Steph, I watched her waste away. Held her hand through chemo, cleaned up when she couldn't make it to the bathroom, pretended everything was fine when she was terrified."

Her hand moved to cup the side of his neck, thumb stroking along his jaw, but she stayed silent.

"When she died, I was ..." His voice cracked completely. "I was nothing. Just this hollow fucking shell walking around pretending to be alive. I didn't know how to be a person anymore without taking care of her."

Tears he hadn't expected began to burn and blur his vision. Stephanie's other hand joined the first, both palms framing his face as she wiped away the tears with her thumbs.

"About a year later, Michelle looked at me one morning and said I was stuck. That I'd lost myself completely when Mom got sick, and she was tired of waiting for me to find my way back."

His breath hitched. Stephanie's hands moved to his shoulders, kneading the tension there. "She said she didn't even know if he could come back. And then she just ... left. Packed her shit and left me sitting in our apartment, wondering if she was right. If Trevor had died with my mom and I just didn't notice."

Trevor described the years that followed, his voice thick with emotion. "I existed. That's all. Went to work, came home, watched TV, went to bed. For fucking years. I felt like I was sleepwalking through my own life, waiting for something to wake me up or kill me, whichever came first."

He wiped at his eyes with his free hand, embarrassed by the tears but unable to stop them. Stephanie's hands moved back to his chest, palms flat against his heart, feeling it race beneath her touch.

"A couple of years later, I found myself booking a singles cruise. I was so desperate to feel something—anything—that I figured maybe I needed to act out being a different person. See if that could shock Trevor back to life."

Her hands slid up to his shoulders again, then down his arms in long, soothing strokes.

"Steve was only supposed to be a one-time thing. Just a jolt of confidence, you know? I didn't plan the details. Just thought I'd try being someone more ... alive. Brighter clothes, bigger energy."

"What happened that first night?" she asked softly, one hand moving to trace along his collarbone while the other rested on his chest.

Trevor's voice broke with wonder and pain mixed together. "People gravitated toward him immediately. They laughed, they remembered his name, they wanted to be around him. For the first time since Mom died, I felt ..." He swallowed hard. "I felt like maybe I wasn't completely dead inside. Like there was still something in me worth loving."

Stephanie's body pressed closer against him, understanding the significance.

"But it didn't stop there," he continued, his voice getting rougher. "It was only supposed to be once. But then … cruise after cruise, Steve became more elaborate, more essential to me, feeling like I was actually alive instead of just … existing."

"How elaborate?" The question was gentle, without judgment. Her hand moved to stroke the back of his neck, fingers threading through his hair.

Trevor's voice dropped with shame and desperation. "I have color-coded costume rotations. I plan Steve's outfits six months in advance. I have spreadsheets. Fucking spreadsheets for a persona I created because I was too broken to be myself."

She pressed a soft kiss to his chest, then another to his collarbone, wordless gestures of acceptance that nearly undid him completely.

"That one-time confidence boost became …" His voice cracked again. "It became the only time I felt like I mattered. The only time I felt like who I used to be before everything went to shit. And I was terrified that without Steve, I'd go back to being that hollow shell Michelle left behind."

The tears were coming freely now, years of buried pain finally finding release. Stephanie's hands moved over his shoulders, down his arms, then back to frame his face, her thumbs wiping away the tears as they fell.

"Some nights I'd lie awake wondering if Trevor was actually gone forever, if Steve was all that was left of me that anyone could love."

When he finished, Stephanie remained quiet for a long moment, her hands still moving over his shoulders as she absorbed everything he'd shared. The loss, the grief, the years of caregiving, the abandonment, and his desperate attempt to feel alive again.

She pushed herself up on her elbows to look directly into his eyes, her own glistening with unshed tears.

"Jesus, Trev," she said, her voice thick with emotion. "No wonder you needed Steve."

Her insight cut straight to the truth. "Michelle sounds like she tried, but ... fuck, Trev. You were grieving. Of course, you weren't the same person."

Her hand cupped his face as she spoke. "But look at you now. You're still funny, you still care about people, you still light up when you talk about things you love. Steve didn't create that. He just gave you a way to let it out again."

She paused, her thumb brushing away a tear. "What you did for your mom isn't shameful. It's love."

"I think Steve is you when you're not afraid to take up space again. When you remember you deserve to be seen."

"You don't have to pick one or the other, you know," she said softly.

Her words hit with enough force to leave him raw. "You think ... Steve is just Trevor amplified?"

"I think Steve is you when you stop being afraid of being too much."

The tears came harder now, and she continued to wipe them away with her thumbs. "I've been so afraid that without Steve, no one would want me."

Stephanie's response was simple, direct, and devastatingly perfect.

"Between you and me, I really like Trevor ... hell, I fell in love with Trevor."

Trevor propped himself up on his elbows to look at her, his eyes searching her face. "You did?"

"Back in college, yeah." She reached up to trace his cheekbone with her thumb. "I was too fucking scared of how I felt, so I kept sabotaging us before we could become anything real. You were never boring, Trev. You were terrifying. Because you made me feel things I wasn't ready for."

Trevor fixed on her, a part of him breaking open. "All these years, I thought I wasn't enough. That you saw right through me and found me ... ordinary."

"You were extraordinary," she said softly. "That was the problem. I was twenty-one and stupid and thought feelings that strong had to be dangerous."

He leaned down to kiss her, gentle and wondering. "And now?"

"Now?" She gave him a wry smile. "Look, Playboy, I'm not gonna say I love you after one night, but I'm definitely not running away this time."

They settled back into each other's arms, Trevor drawing her against him. The silence that had haunted him for nine years transformed into something he'd almost forgotten: peace.

"Thank you," he whispered against her hair. "For seeing me."

"Thank you for letting me," she replied, pressing a soft kiss to his collarbone.

As consciousness began to fade, Trevor rediscovered a feeling he thought lost. It was the peace of being known and wanted exactly as he was. The sound of waves drifted through the open balcony door, carrying them both into sleep, wrapped in love and the promise of morning.

Nine

BANG BANG BANG.

The aggressive knocking jolted Trevor and Stephanie awake like a fire alarm. Trevor's eyes snapped open to find himself still naked, Stephanie curled against his chest, and his electric blue wig lying forgotten on the cabin floor like a discarded costume.

"STEVE!" Cami's voice boomed through the door. "Open this door right now!"

"We know you're in there!" Lila added with theatrical flair. "We can hear shuffling!"

Trevor glanced at the clock on his nightstand; 12:15 p.m. *Fuck!* They'd slept through breakfast and the rest of the morning.

"Don't make us get security!" Cami escalated. "Or worse, tell Maude you're having a breakdown!"

"We've initiated wellness checks!" Lila's voice carried the drama of a breaking news alert. "Nancy's about to organize a search party!"

Trevor sat up, running his hands through his real hair. "I'm alive, I'm fine!"

There was a suspicious pause outside the door.

"You sound weird," Cami said suspiciously. "Are you sick? Depressed? Having an identity crisis?"

"Or ..." Lila's voice sparked with curiosity. "Wait. Do you have someone in there?"

Stephanie pressed her face into the pillow to muffle her laughter, her shoulders shaking against his chest.

"Just ... give me a minute!" Trevor called out desperately.

"A MINUTE?" Cami's outrage could have powered the ship's engines. "Steve, you missed breakfast, you missed morning activities, and now you're being evasive!"

"Oh my God, he totally has someone in there!" Lila's excitement was palpable.

"Stephen!" Cami's voice could have shattered glass. "Are you having a feelings crisis or a sex crisis? Because we're equipped to handle both!"

"Can we not diagnose me through a door?" Trevor pleaded.

"Well, we're heading to lunch at La Dolce Mare," Lila announced. "You're coming, right? Because missing TWO meals is grounds for intervention."

Trevor looked down at Stephanie, who was grinning up at him with sleepy eyes and mussed hair. The choice felt surprisingly easy.

"Actually, I think I'm going to order room service."

The stunned silence outside the door was deafening.

"I'm sorry, WHAT?" Cami's voice cracked. "Since when do you voluntarily choose solitude over socializing?"

"Room service?" Lila's theatrical gasp could have won awards. "Steve, cough twice if you're being held against your will!"

Another pause. Both women are processing this significant change in behavior.

"Wait a minute," Cami said slowly. "You DO have someone in there!"

"I KNEW IT!" Lila's victory cry echoed down the corridor.

" I just ... I need a quiet afternoon," Trevor said evasively.

"Since WHEN?" Cami's voice cracked with disbelief.

"Something is definitely up," Lila declared. "This is not *Steve* behavior."

Trevor could hear muffled whispering outside the door.

"It's got to be Stephanie." Cami's voice was barely audible.

"Oh my God, yes!"

"Stephanie, honey, well done!" Cami called through the door. "We've never seen Steve choose solitude over socializing!"

"Seriously, girl, you've accomplished the impossible!" Lila added.

Stephanie lost her restraint. "Maybe all he needed was to be fucked senseless and left speechless!" she called, her voice ringing with triumph.

Trevor's face went crimson as he buried it in his hands.

"Oh, I already liked you, but now I LOVE you!" Cami's delighted laughter filled the hallway.

"She's got perfect claws! Steve, you better keep this one!" Lila approved.

"Okay, okay, go away now," Trevor called through the door, still mortified.

"Fine, but we're getting details later," Cami declared. "ALL the details."

Their footsteps finally retreated down the corridor.

"Your friends are wonderfully ridiculous," Stephanie said, stretching against him like a satisfied cat.

"They're something, alright." Trevor pressed a kiss to her forehead. "Room service?"

"Definitely."

An hour later, they were lounging on his balcony with plates of fresh fruit and sandwiches, the Caribbean sun warming their skin as the ocean breeze played with Stephanie's hair. She'd borrowed one of his T-shirts, and seeing her in his clothes felt more intimate than all of last night's passion.

"So, what's it like going back to regular life after all this?" she asked, stealing a strawberry from his plate.

Trevor considered the question, watching the endless blue horizon. "Usually feels like stepping back into someone else's skin. But maybe not this time."

"What's regular life like for you anyway? Besides warehouse work."

They talked easily about their respective cities, their jobs, the small details that made up their everyday worlds. Trevor described his modest apartment, his weekend routines, the quiet corners of his life he'd never shared with anyone on a cruise before.

"You seem more relaxed than you were even yesterday," Stephanie observed, her fingers intertwined with his.

"I feel more ..." He searched for the right words. "Like myself."

"Good." Her smile was radiant in the afternoon light. "I like yourself."

As the sun began its descent toward the horizon, Trevor knew they couldn't hide in his cabin forever. "I should probably get ready for tonight's farewell mixer."

"Probably," she agreed, but neither of them moved.

Eventually, though, reality intruded. Trevor stood and stretched, then moved to his closet to choose something appropriate for the evening. Simple but nice. No costume required.

Stephanie watched him from the bed, and when he turned back toward her, she was holding the electric blue wig.

"Ready for the show?" she asked with a knowing smile.

Trevor looked at the wig, then at her, then at himself in the mirror. For nine years, that synthetic hair had been his security blanket, his ticket to belonging, his permission to take up space.

"Nah, not tonight," he said, taking the wig from her hands and tossing it across the room with casual finality. It landed in a puddle of electric blue against the far wall, looking suddenly small and lifeless.

Stephanie stood and ran her fingers through his real hair, tousling the salt-and-pepper strands. "You don't need the wig to be a rock star."

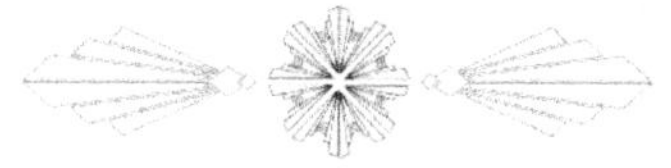

They stopped briefly at Stephanie's cabin so she could change from his borrowed T-shirt into a dress that actually fit. When they arrived at the Topaz Lounge hand in hand, the space was alive with farewell celebration energy. Crystal chandeliers cast rainbow fragments across the jewel-toned décor, and animated conversations filled the air as passengers savored their final night together.

Instead of making his usual grand entrance, Trevor deliberately chose a secluded corner booth where he and Stephanie could slide in side by side and watch the celebration without drawing attention.

Most of the broader Mingle community didn't even notice him arrive. Without the blue hair and glittery costumes, he was just another passenger enjoying the final day.

But Cami and Lila spotted him immediately.

"Well, well, well," Cami announced as she and Lila swooped in, both looking like they'd had very interesting evenings. "Look who's choosing the quiet corner like an actual human being instead of a walking disco ball."

"Okay, but seriously, what's with the hair situation?" Lila demanded, wedging herself into the booth on Trevor's other side with the satisfied ease of a woman who was definitely walking differently today. "Or should I say, lack thereof? You look almost normal."

"Decided to give my scalp an afternoon off," Trevor replied, unconsciously running a hand through his salt-and-pepper hair.

"An afternoon off?" Cami laughed, her statement earrings catching the light as she shook her head. "Honey, that wig has been working overtime for nine years. OSHA should investigate."

"Remember the neon green phase?" Lila grinned wickedly, shifting in her seat with a slight wince that didn't go unnoticed. "You looked like a tropical parrot who'd been electrocuted by a disco."

"You two said you loved that wig!" Trevor protested.

"We lied!" they said in perfect unison, then high-fived over his lap, nearly elbowing Stephanie in the face.

That's when Stephanie's friends descended, converging on the corner booth like sharks who'd scented blood in the water.

"Ladies, ladies!" Becca announced, practically bouncing as she squeezed herself into the booth beside Lila, half in her lap. "Emergency debrief session. Stephanie looks like she just rediscovered what good sex feels like."

"Or maybe she finally got better than married sex," Angela added, dragging over one of the spare chairs and dropping into it with obvious satisfaction. She raised her glass toward Stephanie. "That glow says it all."

Rachel showed up last, taking in the overstuffed booth with open horror. "This is insane. You cannot fit this many people into one booth."

"Sure we can," Lila shot back, patting her thigh. "Come on, counselor. You managed last night."

A chorus of whoops and ooooohs rose from the table as Rachel flushed but slid in anyway, ending up practically perched on Lila's lap.

"You're all ridiculous," Rachel muttered, but her smirk betrayed her.

Stephanie groaned and buried her face in Trevor's shoulder, but he could feel her laughter shaking against him. Cami whooped, Angela clinked her glass, and Becca leaned in like she was courtside at a championship game.

"You actually have really nice hair under there," Rachel said to Trevor, clearly desperate to redirect attention.

"Right? I keep telling him that," Stephanie said, squeezing Trevor's hand with obvious pride. "Much better than that electric cotton candy situation he usually rocks."

"You seem way more ... zen tonight," Cami observed, studying Trevor with professional interest. "Usually, you'd have us all doing jazz hands by now."

"That was one time," Trevor said defensively.

"Fifty-three times, honey," Lila corrected with deadly accuracy. "Graham's developed a permanent twitch."

"Or the time you convinced half the ship to do synchronized swimming in formal wear," Cami added.

"You two are absolutely the worst," Trevor groaned, but he was grinning.

"We're the best and you know it," Lila shot back. "Besides, we're not the ones holding hands like teenagers."

"Speaking of which, Stephanie!" Becca interrupted, her attention suddenly laser-focused. "Girl, on a scale of one to 'call the Coast Guard,' how good was the sex last night?"

"Solid Coast Guard with a side of 'thank God for soundproof cabins,'" Stephanie replied without missing a beat, making Trevor choke on his drink.

"I can relate," Rachel muttered, then immediately turned three shades of red as everyone's attention snapped to her.

"EXCUSE ME?" Stephanie practically shrieked with delight. "Since when do you kiss and tell?"

"Glass house, counselor," Angela added with a wicked grin aimed at Stephanie.

"Speaking of legal matters," Lila purred, "I can confirm that Rachel's briefs were thoroughly examined. Multiple times. For accuracy."

Rachel's face could have powered the ship's navigation lights. "Can we please focus on literally anyone else?"

"Absolutely not," Becca declared. "This is the most interesting Rachel has been since law school. What happened to 'I'm just here to relax and read legal thrillers'?"

"I got … distracted," Rachel mumbled.

"You weren't distracted last night. Or this morning," Lila practically purred. "I prefer 'comprehensively debriefed.'"

"Oh my God, you're both horrible," Rachel laughed despite herself.

"Says the woman who woke me up at 2 a.m. with her tongue," Lila shot back with a grin that could melt steel.

"That was research!"

"Yeah, oral research."

The table erupted in laughter, everyone delighting in the mortified but amused expression on Rachel's face. It was the kind of merciless but loving teasing that only happened between people who genuinely cared about each other.

"Speaking of research," Cami said, wiping tears from her eyes as she gestured toward Trevor, "we've been studying Steve's behavior for nine years, and apparently all it took was one night with the right woman to completely rewire him."

"Turns out your research methods were all wrong," Stephanie said, raising her wine glass with a triumphant grin that made Trevor's ears burn. "Turns out he just needed someone who knew how to ride the equipment properly."

"STEPHANIE," Trevor protested, his face flaming.

"What? I'm not ashamed! Best sex I've had in years, possibly ever, and I'm not even a little bit sorry about it." She raised her glass higher. "Cheers to that!"

The table erupted in cheers and laughter as everyone raised their glasses, except Trevor, who wanted to crawl under the elegant velvet seating.

"Sometimes I question why I live with this torment," he groaned.

"It's what friends are for," Lila agreed solemnly. "Speaking of which, Stephanie, did you actually break the man or just reprogram him?"

"NOPE," Trevor interrupted, standing up so fast he nearly knocked over his chair. "I'm getting another drink. Several drinks. Maybe all the drinks."

"Bring back shots!" Cami called after him.

"I hate all of you!" he called back, but he was laughing.

The lively hum carried on as fresh drinks appeared and the lounge swelled with farewell energy. Trevor, despite his protests, felt assurance grow with every playful jab, every unforced laugh, every signal that these people welcomed him—whether he wore the wig or not.

Then Maude took the stage.

"Ladies and gentlemen," her voice carried easily over the crowd as conversations quieted. The Mingle at Sea host commanded natural attention, her elegant presence drawing everyone's focus.

She began with the traditional farewell words about community and connection, thanking everyone for the friendships formed and memories made during their week together. Yet her tone carried more weight than usual.

Trevor stilled. Maude's pauses felt deliberate, each silence carrying the promise of more to come.

"Before we conclude our voyage," Maude continued, her voice taking on a more ceremonial tone, "we have a very special announcement tonight."

The crowd's interest sharpened, people setting down drinks and paying closer attention.

"We have someone joining the Mingle at Sea Hall of Fame tonight," Maude announced. "Steve, could you come up here?"

She scanned the crowd, her smile expectant. "Has anyone seen Steve tonight?"

"Steve?" voices called out from around the lounge. "Where's Steve?" "I haven't seen him!"

People began actively looking around for the familiar shock of blue hair and bright costumes that had been a fixture of their cruise experience for years.

Trevor's heart hammered against his ribs. They'd planned this for Steve, having no idea about his transformation. He looked at Stephanie, who squeezed his hand encouragingly. Then, at his friends around the table all nodding with supportive smiles.

Trevor stood up.

The movement caught some attention, and he felt people's eyes on him as he made his way through the crowd toward the stage. Double-takes followed in his wake as passengers slowly realized this was Steve, but looking completely different.

"Is that Steve?" he heard someone whisper. "What happened to his hair?"

By the time he reached the stage, a murmur of recognition was rippling through the crowd.

"Steve!" Maude's face lit up with warm surprise. "I almost didn't recognize you without your blue hair!" Her expression softened with understanding. "But then again, the sea looks different at every depth, doesn't it?"

The crowd chuckled, and Trevor felt the familiar spotlight attention, but without the armor of performance. Just himself, standing in front of his cruise family.

"Ladies and gentlemen," Maude continued, "Steve ... nine ... no, ten years of bringing joy, connection, and unforgettable memories to our cruises ... and now the first inductee to the hall of fame."

Cheers and applause swelled around Trevor, the sound thick with love that left him unsteady. This community was his world, and in their eyes, he belonged to them too.

Maude pressed the microphone into his hands. Trevor stood before the room while his chosen family waited, faces glowing with encouragement.

Ten years as Steve. A decade of costumes and performance, protection wrapped in glitter and synthetic hair. Ten years of being loved for playing a part.

But these people weren't applauding just Steve. They celebrated him—every moment of joy he'd created, every friendship he'd nurtured, every bit of community he'd built. Their love transcended the costume.

Trevor smiled, the gesture feeling natural and authentic as he leaned into the microphone.

"Thank you, everyone, but please ... call me Trevor."

About the author

I'm J.D. Harbor, a romance novelist drawn to love stories set on the high seas. A former military photojournalist, I found my writing voice capturing real-life moments in the field. Now, I craft tales of connection, adventure, and self-discovery aboard cruise ships.

My RomantiSea Serenades series begins with Emerald Tide and Sapphire Seas, companion novels following two souls brought together by fate on a cruise. While their romance spans both books, each story delves into one character's personal journey. Inspired by my own experience of meeting my wife on a voyage, these novels embrace the magic of love unfolding when least expected.

Originally from Utah, I now live in Central Florida with my wife and two kids, always dreaming up our next adventure on the open water. I believe the best love stories begin with self-discovery—because only when we truly know ourselves can we fully open our hearts to love.

Emerald Tide & Sapphire Seas

Available Now

Aidan's spent years carrying everyone else's expectations. Harper's built the perfect career that's slowly suffocating her soul. When they both end up on a singles cruise they never wanted to take, the last thing either expects is to find exactly what they've been missing.

He's all quiet loyalty and hidden longing. She's bright ambition wrapped around deep exhaustion. But somewhere between sunrise conversations and stolen moments, they realize that sometimes you have to drift away from shore to discover who you really are.

His story. Her story. One life-changing voyage.

Emerald Tide reveals his journey as a man torn between duty and dreams finally chooses himself. Sapphire Seas shows her path as a burned-out perfectionist learns that the best success stories aren't always the ones that look good on paper.

Ready to set sail? These full-length companion novels will sweep you away on a romance that proves the most beautiful destinations are the ones you never planned to reach.

RomantiSea Serenades: Where voyages of holding on and letting go find safe harbor.

Scarlet Wave & Golden Shores

Coming November 2025

Scarlet's got the perfect life on paper, but she's drowning in her own success. Jerry lives for duty and his two sons, convinced that good fathers don't get to want anything for themselves. Neither planned to board a singles cruise, and they definitely didn't plan to fall for each other.

She's all sharp wit and polished control. He's quiet strength and hidden vulnerability. But somewhere between paddleboard disasters and late night heart-to-hearts, they discover that the best connections happen when you stop trying to stay afloat on your own.

Ready to dive in? This isn't just another shipboard romance. It's one epic love story that'll make waves in your heart.

Two perspectives. One unforgettable romance.

Scarlet Wave gives you her side as a burned out professional learns to sea life differently. Golden Shores shows his journey as a single dad discovers that love doesn't require perfection.

Get the complete story across two full-length companion novels. Trust me, you'll want to stay anchored to this romance from start to finish.

RomantiSea Serenades: Where solo journeys become shared memories.